Battle at Broken Knee

He was a big, nondescript man of the kind you could see anywhere along the rough border of those days and with his old and worn clothes he was clearly unconcerned about his appearance. Little wonder, then, that he was called Careless O'Connor. But first impressions could be deceptive for Careless was a mighty tough *hombre* and a Texas Ranger to boot!

Trouble always seemed to find him and so it was when he came upon a Concord coach with the driver and horses shot dead. But one passenger, Grace Whitfield, was still alive and now it was Careless's mission to find the murdering border ruffians who were responsible for the killings.

His life would be in constant danger as he faced frightening odds. Would even his formidable skills and courage be enough to bring rough justice to the bushwhackers?

Battle at Broken Knee

Gordon Landsborough

A Black Horse Western

ROBERT HALE · LONDON

© 1953, 2004 Gordon Landsborough
First hardcover edition 2004
Originally published as
Careless O'Connor by Mike M'Cracken

ISBN 0 7090 7317 8

Robert Hale Limited
Clerkenwell House
Clerkenwell Green
London EC1R 0HT

The right of Gordon Landsborough to be identified as
author of this work has been asserted by him
in accordance with the Copyright, Designs and
Patents Act 1988.

Typeset by
Derek Doyle & Associates, Liverpool.
Printed and bound in Great Britain by
Antony Rowe Limited, Wiltshire

ONE

STRANGE PARTNERS!

A lone rider saw the buzzards and sent his horse climbing to the top of a giant sandstone bluff, where he could look down over the vast, arid prairie that stretched north to the Neuces River.

He sat there, looking down, man and horse dwarfed by the height of the crumbling red sandstone cliff. Below him was a coach.

'A Concord,' he thought. He saw two horses dead in their harness. 'Two?' He frowned. 'Two hosses ain't no good fer pullin' a coach.'

He wondered at it, his eyes narrowed against the hot, noon-day sun. He'd never seen a coach so far south. The war with Mexico was only just over, with American troops still in occupation of the principal Mexican cities. It made for bitter feeling, and though the political leaders of both countries had signed a treaty of peace, there were men on both

5

sides of the Border who thought only of vengeance. Raids were frequent, and the profession of banditry was common.

After a while the lone rider turned his horse's head and descended to the trail by a circuitous route.

He rode up to the silent coach, piled grotesquely on to those horses. The leather curtains flapped in the glassless window frames, so that he had to pull them aside to peer within, but the coach was empty of passengers. He saw that there was no driver, either, anywhere near the coach. Just two old horses dead in their harness. Shot from close range, probably when they were standing, he thought, seeing the death wounds. Pistol shots.

He was a big, nondescript man on a big, nondescript horse. The kind of man you saw anywhere on the rough Border of those days. His clothes were old and worn, with many a tear in them, and little evidence of patching or mending. His blue shirt didn't have any buttons and was open to catch the comfort of the breeze; his jeans were made from homespun Texas cloth that didn't stand up to hard wear in the saddle, and were out at the knees and on his seat. and his old, sweat-stained hat would have disgraced a tramp.

He didn't seem the kind of man to bother about his appearance, however. His face was so browned by the sun that it was as dark as any Comanche's –

it looked big and flat and hard at first sight; the kind of face you see on a man who's been knocked around. But those narrowed eyes held a glint of humour.

He rolled himself a smoke, and for some reason went riding back along the trail. He never knew himself quite why he did it, except that mysteries always intrigued him, and going back seemed one way of perhaps finding a clue to the mystery of the stranded Concord.

So he came upon the coach-driver. He didn't know that at the time, though. Just off the trail he saw an old man lying under a clump of mesquite.

He knelt beside the man. Saw that he hadn't been shot but looked as though he'd died from a broken neck. He stood up, eyes examining the sign along the trail. He saw where the coach wheels had run into a big rock. Probably that jolt had thrown the old man out of his high seat and he'd broken his neck on hitting the ground, the big *hombre* thought.

He climbed back into his saddle, then sat again and looked round. Treaties between governments meant nothing to starving mestizos over in Mexico, and sometimes they came flooding, a savage, nearly naked horde under their broad sombreros, into Texas.

So he looked back, and when he was sure there were no fleet-footed Mexican ponies descending the canyon, he went trotting his big, unlovely brown horse along the trail northwards.

And again he didn't know why he did it. It wasn't the way he wanted to go, anyway – he was simply acting on hunches. And one of his hunches was that right now he was under observation, and he didn't like it and he wanted to know more about the unseen watcher.

So when his mount blew suddenly through its distended nostrils and evinced a desire to shy away from a clump of thorn scrub, the big, casual-looking *hombre*'s eyes at once went to it, questioning.

He tried to push his horse towards the thorns, but the intelligent beast went circling away, and that told him there was something lying up in the grasses – something or someone.

He was too wary to get off his horse, and he fought it with one hand and made it sidle close up to the bushes. Then he saw—

There was a heel. Just that sticking up among the grasses. He saw nothing else. He sat and looked at it a long time, and it never moved, so he got out of his saddle and slowly ambled up to the grasses. When he stood over the heel he saw a body lying in the cover. Jeans and a faded check shirt of Louisiana cotton.

He saw blonde curls in the grasses, and a black, velvet ribbon that tied them back. A girl!

His face went harder than the blued barrel of his Sharps, looking down at that stiff, slim figure. Along this Border death was no stranger to him, but his instincts as a man were outraged and shocked when death came to a girl. A young girl, a

8

pretty girl, he thought, going down on one knee.

His hands touched her thin shirt and he felt warmth under it. That touch of his hand triggered things off, apparently. She reared up and round at his touch. And she had a gun.

She was young, she was pretty. She had a brown face like his own, a face bronzed by the sun of Texas. She had eyes that were bluer than the skies above – intelligent eyes in an intelligent face. But there was horror in them, and fear of death and worse than death as they came round and looked on to his big, flat, fist-battered face.

He saw the gun lifting, though the slim brown hand trembled. It was a woman's gun, a baby Derringer. But he couldn't fire on a woman. He went diving over the top of her, grabbing for the gun as he did so.

His fingers gripped it and pulled it away, but the action got the hammer triggering down and the gun exploded in his hand.

His weight never touched her. He rolled beyond her in the dry, stalky grasses, still gripping that Derringer, then he came rolling lithely to his feet, though he was a big man.

He was in time to see the girl leaping away from him, and she looked long-legged as she raced through the grass, her men's pants tight upon her. The big *hombre* saw she was headed for his horse, and blasted off a whistle through his clenched teeth. It startled his horse, that sudden, blasting sound, and it came plunging up on its hind legs, and the girl missed the curb rein by a couple of yards. By the time the horse was down, the man had grabbed the girl and was saying, 'What d'you think you're doin' with my hoss, lady?'

She hammered at him with her fists, shouting, 'Let me go! Keep away from me.' And she was terrified.

He stood and looked at her. She heard a voice that drawled and it said, in mild astonishment. 'You sure are het up. What're you so scared about?'

His eyes lifted beyond the girl. Without hesitation he dived at her, caught her and threw her down on the ground. She hadn't time to cry out with fear. The second they hit earth, he fell away from her, came up with his Sharps and began to fire.

She came up on all fours, trembling, not knowing what it all signified. He shouted, 'Keep down – Mexes!'

A bullet sang close to her face, and she went down. She rolled over on to her back and watched the crouching form of the big man dark against the blue summer sky.

He fired steadily, and the smoke plumed down and got into her nose. Somehow his calmness had an effect upon her and she began to take a grip on herself.

She lifted her head and looked round. The mestizos, those oppressed peons who were in revolt all along the Border against gringos and their own avaricious government alike, were circling round at a distance. There were about fifteen of them, though two or three were riding away as if they were hurt.

She heard the big man's drawl, very cheerful and unhurried: 'They didn't expect ter run into a Sharps repeater.' He squinted along the sights, then fired.

She saw the swirl of movement as the shot went home. A man cried out in pain, and then went riding slowly away, huddled over the neck of his bare-backed pony. All the other Mexicans scattered, then rode round and came together to parley a good distance away.

The girl heard the big fellow say, complacently, 'They think they're outa range, but I could knock 'em off like sittin' ducks even at twice this distance.'

The girl considered his remark, then forced her dry mouth into shaping a question. 'Why – don't you?'

He finished reloading, then grounded the butt and looked at her. He drawled, 'They're starvin', them poor galoots. That's what makes 'em ride north – food.'

'Not revenge?'

'Mebbe revenge, too.' He sighed, as if he didn't think revenge worth much. 'They've had war on their land fer the last coupla years, with first the Mexican army eatin' up all the food they could lay hands on, an' then a United States army doin' the same thing. It's ruined 'em, ranchero an' peon alike. Now hunger sends 'em raidin' into Texas, in the hope they c'n run off a few head o' beeves, so they c'n eat or mebbe start buildin' up herds agen.'

She listened to that slow, comfortable voice. It was more soothing than anything she had known before, even with a savage enemy circling no more than two hundred yards away.

He looked at her, and there was a little grin on his face. 'You've kinda forgotten to be scared of me now,' he said.

She looked at the Mexicans. They had reined in a short line down opposite where the coach lay. Any moment she expected them to charge.

She touched his arm, frightened. 'Look, they're going to attack us again.'

The big *hombre* just looked at the mestizos, then shook his head. 'Not on your life, ma'am. They won't attack a feller with a Sharps repeater; they know they haven't a chance. You watch 'em clear out when we ride towards 'em.' And she thought he said something about them wanting 'beef more'n scalps.'

He stood, concerned, then put his hand on her shoulder in a gesture that was rough, but intended to be consoling. 'You're still scared?' His eyes lifted and sought the thorn scrub. 'Reckon you went through hell, lyin' doggo all that time in the bushes, huh?' That would be enough to break anyone's nerve, having to lie out in this heat, while an enemy searched for you. And he could see there had been a search, because of the criss-crossing of tracks all along the trail-side.

She had pluck, and tried to pull herself together. 'I'm sorry,' she gulped. 'But – I've had a day of it.' Her eyes lifted in horror, remembering back. 'In Broken Knee, they were frightening. Then Jim went away and didn't come back, and I was told to pull out of town as—'

'Jim?'

My brother.'

Startled, she found herself being lifted and swung into the saddle. He came up easily behind her. That was something she was beginning to notice about this casual-looking *hombre* – how easily, how swiftly he moved.

'What happened after that?' Fascinated, she realised that he was turning his mount into a walk directly towards the hostile Mexicans.

'Some of the younger men came after us.'

He didn't understand it. She didn't say any more because she was watching those Mexicans. They turned slowly and began to walk their ponies towards the shadowy canyon. Her relief was tremendous.

'How come that coach got here?'

He couldn't get over that, a stage coach right alongside the Border.

She seemed surprised. 'That Concord?' It was his turn to be astonished. 'That's mine, I own it.'

He looked sharply down on to her blonde curls, flying in the wind. Then his eyes strayed off into the mesquite, where that old man lay. He asked,

13

softly, 'That your paw out there?' Because he knew it couldn't be her brother.

She said, 'No, I don't know him. He was just driving for me.'

The big *hombre* sighed. When they came up to the wrecked coach he swung down and lifted her out of the saddle. She came easily, as though he didn't notice her weight much.

They stood together, listening to the hollow echo of unshod hoofs along the canyon. They were fading; the danger from the Mexicans had gone.

He said, 'Ma'am, I ain't usually nosey, but what you say kinda makes me curious. Mebbe we could make coffee, an' while I rustle up a drink you c'n tell me what you want me to know.'

The girl pulled open the coach door and sat on the floor, her feet outside but her head and body in the shade. She looked at him and thought he was a man to be trusted, so she told him the story.

He fixed a little fire, using dried dung from the trail, then boiled coffee. He was working, listening attentively, but she realised after a time that for all his casual air he was keeping incessant watch all around them, and his Sharps was always within inches of his hand.

'Last year my father died, leaving my brother and me on our own in MacAlester in Oklahoma. Jim's only a couple of years older than me, and inclined to be – well, impulsive. He got restless after Father died, and was always talking about moving into Texas and becoming a rancher. But it

14

needs money to buy land and stock and last out two or three years, and we didn't have all that to play with.'

'So?'

She laughed, as if now she looked back, she, too, could see a funny side to things. 'So he went out and bought a stagecoach.' She saw the incredulous expression on the big, flat, browned face and nodded, still laughing. 'He did – though I guess someone smart talked him into it. One day he came home with a coach and two horses, all that we could afford, and full of the prospects of starting a stagecoach company somewhere along the border. He said that the fellow who'd sold him the coach swore there was a fortune to be made, operating even a single coach.'

The big *hombre* poured out coffee into a mug for her, but drank from the pot himself. Politely he said, 'Fortunes seem easily made – when you're young an' green.'

'We were green.' She nodded, then sipped appreciatively. She said, 'I didn't realise how thirsty I was. It must be hours since I last drank.' The shadows were back in those blue eyes at the memory.

'The trouble was, we couldn't find a place that didn't seem served with a coach line. Always some-one had thought of it before us. So we came on to the Border territory, because we knew people were just returning to their homes after the war, and we thought this time there wouldn't be people ahead of us.

'We came into Broken Knee last night!'

She swung round on the big fellow squatting on his heels in the dust, his floppy hat stuck at the back of his head to shade his neck. Her eyes were bewildered, 'I still can't understand it. When we got into Broken Knee a lot of tough-looking men came and told us to beat it. They just said Broken Knee could do without stage coaches a while longer, and gave us till night to pull out.'

'Did you?'

'No.' She shook her blonde head. Her face was filled with fear and anxiety. Her eyes came up and met his. 'My brother said he was going to stop just as long as he wanted. Well, we stayed overnight. At least I did, sleeping in the coach.'

'Jim?' he asked softly.

'I don't know what happened to Jim.' Her voice was tremulous. 'He went out to make inquiries in the town, just after sunset, and he didn't come back. I sat up all night with a shotgun on my lap. but no one came to disturb me. This morning I went round to try to find a sheriff—'

The big man's head came up from his coffee. 'A sheriff? In Broken Knee?' His voice was incredulous, as if he knew such things didn't go together.

She glanced at him. 'You seem to know the place. No, mister, there was neither sheriff nor town marshal. Just no law at all. Then that same crowd came back, hitched up my horses and told

16

me to get moving out of the town. They were nasty looking, and I was scared, so I thought I'd move on until I could tell a sheriff somewhere – say at Neuces Bend – about Jim and get him to look for him.'

The big *hombre* commented. 'You weren't headin' fer Neuces Bend thisaway, ma'am – only fer trouble.'

She nodded. 'I just pulled out of town. I was so worried about Jim, I don't think I was paying much attention to the trail, and I must have taken the wrong fork. Soon after leaving Broken Knee I saw an old man tramping along. He called out for a lift, and offered to drive for me. He seemed a decent man, down on his luck, and I was glad of company. He told me to head for Laredo, when he heard my story because of the Rangers there. He'd just taken the reins from me when we saw half a dozen horsemen coming quickly out from the town after us.' She shivered. 'They were young fellows. That old man recognised them and said they were up to no good. He said they were coming after me, most likely, for – for a bit of sport.'

The big man swilled the grains out of the pot, but was silent. He knew what was in the girl's mind. Those young reckless Border ruffians wouldn't have been nice if they'd got hold of the girl.

'So?'

'The old man told me to drop off the coach and hide in the scrub. He said he'd go on as far as he could and lead them away from me. He was a good man and didn't consider his own danger. So I dropped off by that thorn scrub and lay hidden while they rode past. I watched after the coach and saw that man come out of the seat and fall into the brush. I suppose he was shot.'

'Nope.' The big *hombre* was unbuckling the harness and dragging it off the dead horses. 'A big stone must have made the coach bump, an' it threw him on to his head an' broke his neck, I reckon.'

She whispered. 'Oh dear! I feel it was all my fault.'

'He didn't feel anything.' The big man looked around, then crawled under the sagging coach and began to rope up a broken leather suspension strap.

'They looked around for me, but for some reason missed me when they came to search that patch of thorns. Then two of them rode to where my horses were standing and brutally killed them.

'I didn't dare come out from cover for a while, because I thought one of them might be staying behind to catch me when I did. And then I saw a horseman sitting high up on that sandstone bluff. He looked to be watching for me, and I didn't like his looks.'

The big *hombre* said. 'It was me.' And when she looked embarrassed he merely said, kindly, 'But I don't blame you. Guess I do look a bit of a rough-neck.'

18

She saw him hitch a rope from his saddle to either end of the coach's front axle. She watched in surprise.

'What are you going to do with that coach?' she asked.

'I aim ter buy a share in your proposed new stage line, ma'am,' he said gently. 'I figger you'll need four horses, an' I guess I've got the money to buy 'em.' His head came up sharply. 'Wouldn't you like me for a pardner, ma'am?' he demanded with curious abruptness.

She felt bewildered. She said: 'Yes, I suppose—'

Then she asked desperately: 'But what stage line? From where to where?'

And he said gently: 'From Neuces Bend to Broken Knee.'

She said: 'Broken Knee!' incredulously, and then sat down, unable to believe her ears.

TWO

DAGO-LOVER!

She watched him take a double hitch round the horn of his saddle. He went so casually about his work, never hurrying and doing everything with the minimum of effort.

She said, 'Don't you understand, they don't want stage coaches running into Broken Knee?'

She heard him drawl, 'That's how I figgered things. But mebbe we c'n make 'em change their minds.' Again she noticed the light of humour in his grey eyes. He said, 'Mebbe we'd better get ter know each other, ef we're gonna run as pardners, ma'am.'

'I'm Grace Whitfield.'

'That's a good name,' he told her approvingly. 'It kinda fits you,' he said seriously.

'And your name?'

'O'Connor.' She had a feeling she'd heard the name somewhere along this Border, but couldn't remember in what context. He looked down at his dishevelled attire and said, 'Folks kinda call me Careless – Careless O'Connor.'

She understood. And she said just as he had said, 'The name kind of fits you!' And then they both laughed together.

The big tramp of a cowboy stood back admiring the dilapidated coach. He said, 'I've always kinda wanted to drive a coach. Now I'm gonna get a chance, looks like.'

She asked him where they were going.

'Neuces Bend.' He looked at the buzzards. 'I've got a job ter to,' he announced and walked across to where the dead coach driver lay. He kicked off lumps of earth from the edge of a dried water-course and piled them in a cairn above the unfortunate man to protect his body against the birds. Then he came back to the girl.

He wanted her to sit inside the coach, but she said if he was sitting on top she wanted to be with him.

That's how Neuces Bend saw them – a big, rough-looking man and a bonny fair-haired girl, riding in on a coach behind a horse that was as much a tramp as its master. The sight brought people to the doors, sucking their teeth and watching in silence.

It was that kind of a place, Neuces Bend – the kind of place where men sucked their teeth and said nothing, but watched and never missed a thing.

The town had been Mexican and 'dobe, a place of blank walls and smells and narrow alleys that were made for skulduggery.

Grace had talked about finding an hotel, or, at least, a boarding-room, but big Careless O'Connor shook his head and said they wouldn't find anything like that in Neuces Bend.

Fixing sounded easy. Careless found that since his last visit, Neuces Bend had become flooded with settlers, all anxious to return to the lands they'd held before Santa Anna's Mexican army poured across the Rio Grande and drove them out of Southern Texas.

He left Grace sitting in the coach while he explored in the 'dobe quarter. When he came climbing back on to the new street of clapboard buildings it was to hold his thumbs down, signifying no luck to the girl. She came walking along to meet him. He thought she looked good – young and fresh and lithe and handsome.

He drawled, 'No luck, Gracie. There ain't no place down there that we c'n camp in.'

Grace told him she'd had a visitor while he was away. 'There's another woman in the town – Cathy Wrigley. She and her husband, Ben, have started a general store in one of the new wooden buildings.'

Careless asked quickly: 'Can she put you up?' And the girl nodded, pleased. He said, 'That's good. It's better you should stay with another woman.'

Grace fell into step beside the big, trampish cowboy.

'Cathy says Neuces Bend needs a carrier service to San Dolorosa, down the Neuces. She says the town's crying out for goods, and there aren't many wagons of any kind to bring them in.'

'Meanin' ter make it a freight line?'

'There'll be mail and passengers, too.'

'Okay,' he said tolerantly. 'We'll start runnin' ter San Dolorosa – once we've fixed a service into Broken Knee.'

She stopped, there in the sunny, dusty street and looked up at him with startled eyes. 'But why, Careless? Why ask for trouble when it seems we can get by without it – by starting a line down river and not west along it?'

She heard his gentle voice say, 'You've forgotten – you've a brother lost in Broken Knee. Ef you want news of him, we've got to go back there, an' I figger runnin' a line into the place is one way of goin' back an' findin' out somethin' about it.'

The girl lifted her eyes to his, and they were uncertain, doubting and troubled. Because she felt certain that he was only making her brother an excuse to operate into Broken Knee. She suddenly realised that he had his own reasons for being interested in the town, and it was nothing to do with Jim's disappearance.

Gallantly she smiled, though. 'What about you, Careless?'

'Me? You mean sleepin'?' He looked at the crazy old coach. 'That place'll sleep me fine. It'll be like livin' in the best hotel in Houston, I reckon.'

He walked across and inspected it approvingly. 'Guess my feet'll kinda poke out through the window ef I want ter stretch, but that won't hurt 'em.'

He worked fast. He bought four horses from an immigrant who needed money for stock, before nightfall, and got Grace on the job of drawing up bills to advertise the new coach service into Broken Knee. Then he got into trouble.

Ben Wrigley saw it all, in the shack that served the shattered town as saloon and liquor parlour. Later, he told his wife and Grace about it, and he was troubled.

Grace had taken the big tramp along to meet her new friends, and she'd gone all feminine and fussy, inside the Wrigleys' home, and had wanted to put buttons on his shirt and mend the tears in his pants. Big Careless O'Connor had stuck it for some time, then he'd got tired and growled, 'C'mon, Ben. Let's go get ourselves around a drink.'

Inside the low-ceilinged saloon there'd been the usual collection of desiccated souls mopping up the liquor. It was noisy. Very noisy.

Then one puncher got too drunk and departed from the Texas code of not sticking a nose into other people's business. And he picked on this stranger to town, big Careless O'Connor, as his mark.

Careless, one big foot stuck on an empty barrel by the cool, open doorway, tilting back in a chair which creaked a dislike of the treatment, saw a long brown face, with alcoholic bright eyes shoving up close to him. The face was saying things at him, so Careless shoved it away with a hand almost the size of the barrel top.

Then he got up, hitching his pants up and said, 'You c'n say that again, brother.'

His voice was loud and cold, and it bit into the ears of every man in that saloon, and that room stopped being noisy immediately. The lean, hard, bow-legged cowboy swayed on his small, high-heeled boots. He was a dandy, with a silver-worked gunbelt that looked like loot from an ill-fated haciendado.

That was big Careless O'Connor's first thought, looking at that belt. This *hombre* had been in Mexico, raiding, and it interested him.

The cowboy said it again: 'You're O'Connor, ain't you? The same O'Connor that got pulled outa the Rangers down Oaxaco way?'

Ben Wrigley watched that big man's flat, brown, fighting face. It registered nothing, but the eyes were careful to keep watch on the puncher.

He growled, 'I'm O'Connor!' Then demanded, 'What'n heck's it got ter do with you, fellar?'

'There was a fellar went with the Rangers right

down south into Mexico. He got sent back home fer gettin' ter like the Mexes too much.' There was a pause. Men didn't talk like this and go on living, not when they were speaking to a tough *hombre* who looked as if he knew how to use his two guns.

The big, casual looking fellow asked with studied politeness, 'You got anythin' else inside that mouth you want to ask, brother?'

The silver-belted puncher snarled, 'You heard me ask it. Are you O'Connor, the dago-lover?'

He wasn't drunk any longer, danger whisking the alcohol fumes out of his brain. And he was crouching, the crouch of the professional gunman, knees slightly bent and feet braced apart, arms held away from the side ... and hands claw-like and gripping air within inches of the butts of his ornamented guns.

Big Careless's eyes flickered and saw the crouch of the other man's two companions. They wanted trouble; these were the kind of men who provoked gunfights for the love of seeing men reel and die before their reeking Colt muzzles. Vicious men – troublemakers and no-goods. But Careless had met their kind before.

'You kinda want trouble, don't you?' His eyes travelled from face to face. Back of the gunmen the audience was still trying to hold its breath. The fireworks were about to begin, they guessed.

'Okay, I am O'Connor of the Texas Rangers. I was down Oaxaco, an' I was sent back to Laredo.' He didn't add more to the story, deliberately. He

27

just said, 'Now what're you gonna make of that?'

The middle gunman snarled, 'Greaser lover!' And followed the insult with a downward sweep of the hand.

Big Careless kicked the empty barrel on to the gunnie's knees. The gunnie came out with his guns, but the shock of pain as the barrel rode against him sent him sprawling forward across it. His guns roared off involuntarily, and the bullets plugged the floor.

Big Careless lunged, following the kick at the barrel. The other gunnies hadn't been so swift in going for their guns, and he grabbed one and slammed him on to his companion on the barrel, then started to jump towards the third *hombre*.

Careless saw he was too late. The man was too far back, and he was going for his guns, and there was no time for Careless to leap across and stop him.

The audience saw Careless begin to fall sideways, like a massive tree that had been suddenly felled. And as he went down towards the dirty floorboards, two big fists climbed down on to butts, two hands grasped Colts and pulled them out and levelled them and two fingers tripped hammers on to cartridges that sent bullets speeding across to the third gunman.

White smoke plumed, and the hot gunpowder fumes seemed to saturate the night air. The crash of those Colts on top of the first gunman's seemed to jar the wooden building and set it to vibrate with sound. As the echoes died, they saw Careless's last opponent reel away, hands stiff and empty of guns and seemingly nerveless.

Careless rolled and came on to his feet. The other two gunnies were climbing up off that barrel. The big man stuffed his guns into his holsters and helped them up. He picked the first gunman up, threw him around in his hands, until they heard teeth rattling, and then tossed him clean through the door and out into the dark night beyond.

The second gunman still hadn't got as far as grasping his guns, and he came up swinging. Careless stopped a few solid, tearing blows on his face, but it looked to the audience as if it hurt the fists more than that big countenance. Then he whaled into the gunman.

He came in swinging, and he hit him upstairs, then downstairs and every time his mighty fist landed it seemed that the gunnie's eyes popped inches out of his head in shock of pain. Careless slammed him on the jaw and that was the end of that galoot.

Big O'Connor looked round. Saw a row of heads back of the bar. He said casually: 'We don't want these guys here do we – fightin' an' makin' trouble?' No one thought to argue against that, so Careless stooped and picked up the limp figure of his last opponent and slung him out on to the dusty street as if he were a rag doll. Then he looked at the wounded *hombre*.

'Vamos, brother,' he urged gently, and the gunman vamoosed without any further encouragement.

That night while Careless slept with his big bare feet stuck out through the coach window for coolness, Ben told the womenfolk of the incident.

He was an unhappy man. 'He seems a good guy, that big, tramp of a puncher. He's got humour, an' the fellar's got brains back of that big pan of a face of his. But—' He shrugged. 'A fellar's a no-good ef he's been thrown outa the Rangers. That's like sayin' he's a renegade. What do you think, Grace?'

The girl was twining and untwining her fingers.

'I don't know,' she whispered. 'I don't want to think of him as a renegade – as a dago-lover.' Her eyes lifted to them 'But I can't forget what happened when we ran into a bunch of Mexes. He didn't shoot to kill. In fact, he seemed to be sorry for them.'

Cathy said gently: 'What's wrong in a man behaving like that? All this killing's got to stop sooner or later, and perhaps Careless has seen that ahead of most of us. I like the big tramp.'

Ben said, 'Sure, sure, Cathy, I c'n see your point about not wanting ter kill unnecessarily. But—' He sighed unhappily. 'He got pulled outa the Rangers. He musta done somethin' bad – real bad – to deserve that. I'd like to know what it was.'

When the town awoke next morning it was to find big Careless O'Connor lazing his way around the streets, sticking up the bills that Grace had printed the previous evening.

This morning neither leg of his jeans was tucked inside his riding-boots; he looked bigger, rougher than ever. But he had shaved. People were soon to notice that – that no matter how careless he was in other respects about his appearance, yet he rarely failed to shave.

He stood back, after clumping the last bill to a balcony support and admired his handiwork. He read:

THE WHITFIELD-O'CONNOR STAGE CORPORATION.

A service will be run twice a week to and from Broken Knee and Neuces Bend. Freight and passenger rates by arrangement. Apply Miss Whitfield down at Wrigleys'. First trip out on Wednesday.

Careless was proud of that notice. 'She sure is a smart gal with a pencil, that Gracie Whitfield,' he thought.

Cathy had a breakfast ready for him when he came shoving his big brown pan of a face into the kitchen. She smiled agreeably when he came in. Cathy anyway, hadn't any doubts about the man. But bonny, blonde Grace Whitfield couldn't meet his eyes because of the doubts and thoughts that were in her mind. She murmured greetings, but didn't say much afterwards. If he noticed anything, big Careless didn't show it. He joked lazily, flattered Cathy outrageously, then drifted out to help Ben.

They didn't see him for the rest of the day, not until close on sundown. When he came in Cathy fussed about him and made him some fresh coffee.

Careless stuck it for a time, then wandered into the little improvised kitchen out at the back, where Cathy cooked over a wood stove.

He said carefully: 'Gracie's kinda sore at me, I figger?'

Cathy pushed back a strand of dark, wavy hair. When she looked at him her eyes were calm and dispassionate. 'You don't kill enough Mexicans, Careless, that's your trouble.'

Careless's eyes shot wide open. 'I don't—' he began to exclaim.

'That's how Gracie sees it.'

Cathy turned the beans and bacon on to a chipped, enamel plate. 'She's unhappy, Careless, because of what people think of you.'

He picked up the plate, thinking, and turned towards the door. Cathy was at his elbow, smiling up at him.

He heard her say, 'I don't care what people say about you, you big hobo. I think you're all right!'

He shrugged carelessly. 'Me, I don't give a damn what people say – after that.' Cathy laughed and went in ahead of him.

Careless looked at bonny Grace Whitfield, and

32

he was thinking hard behind that impassive countenance. While he ate he told them of his day's
successes. They hadn't been many.

'I went round town, tryin' ter drum up trade.
There wasn't a fellar would risk sendin' a mule's
ears through ter Broken Knee,' he said cheerfully.
'They all opine it's suicide; they say Broken Knee
jes' naturally don't want stage lines an' sheriff's an'
town marshals an' sich-like. Not right now. I
wanted a fellar ter drive the coach in, too, but I
wasn't exactly trodden on by volunteers.'

Grace looked at him quickly. 'Aren't you driving
it yourself? I thought you said you'd always wanted
to sit up there and drive a Concord?'

Big Careless's grin swept round on to her. He
spoke gently, as he often did. 'Someone drives, an'
someone sits an' holds a gun. That's how stages is
run in these parts, ma'am.'

'You'll hold the gun,' Gracie said and then she
found some spirit. 'And don't you start calling me
ma'am again. It doesn't sound friendly like.'

Careless sighed and said, 'I figgered you wasn't
exactly bein' friendly towards me today, Gracie.
Mebbe that's why it slipped out.'

Grace looked at him, as if his words gave her a
shock. She had probably not realised that her
thoughts – and emotions – were so plain to read.
Careless saw her flush with embarrassment, and he
tried to help her by saying, 'That's all right, Gracie.
Mebbe you're not feelin' up to the mark after
yesterday.'

33

Then his eyes twinkled as he looked at that bonny face, with the becoming tinge of pink and the shining eyes, and he rose. 'Gracie,' he said, 'you come with me. I need someone ter help me drive that coach into Broken Knee. I figger ef the boys hereabouts see another of their bosses we'll mebbe have a queue to jine the firm!'

Grace went red, and red-headed Ben added to the confusion with raucous laughter. Cathy followed Careless out through the door and said, 'You mustn't make fun of Grace, Careless. She's young and she's falling in love with you, you big no-good!'

Careless's mouth went wide with shock. He was a very worried man when slim, blonde, attractive Grace came out to join him. He saw she had changed into a cool summer dress of printed cotton, and he gasped, seeing her for the first time not wearing those faded old jeans.

As they walked down the street he kept watching her sideways, and she must have felt it, for she walked with eyes held straight before her and her face was unusually red, even without the dying rays of the sun upon her.

So at length, he sighed and said weakly, 'I never knew you could look like this, Gracie. You're – gee, you're a peach!'

34

THREE

THE BOSS!

The saloon was beginning to fill up. Careless eyed the men in turn. They weren't very friendly. No one wanted to be seen speaking to a man who bore the brand of renegade, not so soon after the bitterness of the war with Mexico.

Careless didn't come farther than the doorway, but they could hear him clearly from there. His slow drawl, the words even-spaced and good-tempered, complained, 'All day I've bin tryin' ter get some young fellar with sand ter help me start a coach line into Broken Knee. I ain't had much success. I'm wonderin' though, if mebbe some o' you might have changed your minds about workin' fer me an' my pardner, Miss Whitfield.'

Grace's cheeks were flushed; she had a feeling

that the men knew what big Careless O'Connor was doing – knew he was displaying her charms as an inducement for some man to team up with them.

When no one spoke, Careless shrugged and shoved back that disgraceful, floppy-brimmed stetson of his, and drawled, 'Okay. I reckon there ain't much sand left in Texas nowadays....'

He was still talking when a tall, lithe young Texan slapped down his cards and stood up. He was a kid, but tough as they come. He had blue eyes like chips of frozen sky in a face that was lean and brown and handsome. And he had guts.

He hitched up his belt and stalked right up to big Careless O'Connor and said in his face, 'I reckon ter have quite a bit o' sand in me, O'Connor.'

And then, deliberately, offensively, he rapped, 'I don't like ter work fer a Santa Anna man, but fer Blue Eyes here, I'll drive a coach through ter Hades an' back!'

There was a gasp from the crowd at his words. They expected an explosion. Grace expected it, too!

The young Texan was crouching, arms hooked back ready for a lightning draw. But Careless was completely relaxed. He merely said mildly, 'Son, ef you're offerin' ter work fer me pardner, you're took on.'

Big Careless stood there, his hand outstretched,

but the young Texan deliberately ignored it. Instead he grinned, swept off his hat and held out his hand to Grace.

'I'm Burt Clay – Yippee Clay to my friends?' He was smiling boldly, confidently.

'Yippee?' repeated Grace doubtfully. He was shaking her hand, and she felt embarrassed by the naked admiration in his eyes. Yet big, watchful Careless saw that she wasn't displeased by it. 'Will you come to Wrigley's store tomorrow morning, Mr Clay, ready to drive out with – with my pardner?'

Deliberately the cocky young puncher turned his back on big Careless as he said, 'Fer you, ma'am, I'll do even that.'

Grace grabbed her partner and pulled him out through the batwing doors. She was terrified, certain that ultimately there would be fireworks.

But out on the dusty street, Careless asked mildly, 'What're you scared about, Gracie?'

Her words came out in a succession of quick flows. 'That Clay man – he was determined to pick a quarrel with you. I was afraid . . . someone might get hurt.'

'Me – or that cocky young so-and-so?'

She didn't answer. He slipped his hand under her soft warm arm, and she didn't attempt to pull away. His strength always seemed to bind her to him. It was hard to think that such a man should be counted a renegade.

The town turned out to watch the coach make its first trip to Broken Knee, the following morning. The flies were buzzing around the heads of the four drooping horses.

Ben came out with a bucket to give them a last-minute drink, and then Careless and Yippee Clay climbed up on to the high seat. Careless took the reins; young Clay sat nursing a Henry breechloader.

It was an empty trip. They weren't taking so much as a letter, though folks did say that quite a bit of business could be done with the neighbouring town. But then nobody expected success from this trip.

Ben had told Grace that others had thought of running a coach into Broken Knee, and those who hadn't been warned off had been shot up when they tried to run into the town.

She had been bewildered. 'Who are these people who want to keep Broken Knee in such isolation?'

Ben didn't know – not much, anyway. 'Oh, jes' fellars, I reckon. Some gamblin' men, some deserters from the American Army when it was down this way, an' a lot of no-goods who start ter run the moment they see a sheriff's star. They like Broken Knee 'cause it's safe, so they aim ter keep it that way, I reckon. They've got together, and they run the town.'

Big Careless, doing chores for Cathy, had heard. Now his drawling voice butted into the conversation. 'I figger there's more to it than just that, Ben. I figger there's someone back of them two-bit crooks an' gamblers, someone bandin' 'em together ter hold down the honest citizens.' And then his voice had gone very soft! 'An' that means there's somethin' big behind it all. You wouldn't have an idea of anythin' big goin' on in Broken Knee, Ben now, would you?'

Ben jerked his head up, surprised. 'Me, no.'

But half an hour later, Ben said abruptly, 'Queer things happen around here, Careless.'

'Yeah?'

'Every now an' then a lot o' wild young fellars suddenly pull outa their jobs an' go an' ride into Broken Knee. Sometimes we don't see 'em for two-three weeks, then they come back an' spend a lot o' money. Then, all of a sudden, off they go agen. There's some more gunnies quit their jobs today an' took the trail ter Broken Knee; I saw 'em ride through first thing this mornin'.'

Cathy looked troubled. 'You might be running into a lot of trouble, Careless. Why not postpone your first trip – or run one through to San Dolorosa?'

'Because,' big Careless said gently, 'I kinda like the idea of goin' into Broken Knee.'

When he took his seat up on the coach Careless eased off the foot brake and wrestled with the lead horses to get them facing out of town. Grace called, 'Good luck, boys,' and waved to them, and her face was anxious.

Careless stood up, crying out to his horses and sending the long lash cracking a couple of feet above their heads.

They tossed their manes and dug their hoofs into the soft trail sand and the coach started to move. There was a murmur from the crowd, but it wasn't a cheer. Careless knew the crowd didn't give much for his chances of survival on this trip.

He turned and waved to the girls, and then they were drawing steadily out on to the prairie trail. They rode for a time in silence, then Careless got out his makings and, one-handed, rolled himself a cigarette. When he'd licked the paper he proffered the sack of Bull Durham to the young Texan by his side.

Yippee said coldly, 'I've got my own,' and made up from his own sack.

The tall young Texan struck a match and drew smoke into his lungs. Insolently he said, 'You'd better know how we stand, Careless. I take nothin' from a renegade. I'm workin' for Miss Whitfield, not you.'

Careless sighed. There had to be a showdown, he thought, so he said gently, 'Son, I kinda get tired of this renegade talk. Next time I have it from you, you young fire-eater, I'll beat your ears so close together there won't even be room fer your nose in between.'

The young Texan stared. There was something in the way the big man spoke that showed he meant what he said.

Two hours later they came rolling down from the scrub near-desert of the mesa towards the more fertile basin of the Neuces River. Built right on the river bank was Broken Knee, an unlovely huddle of buildings little better than Neuces Bend.

Their arrival was expected. Careless had known it would be and he had wanted it like that so that there could be a showdown. As the four horses came pulling against the brakes down the hill into the 'dobe and frame building cattle town, they saw a reception committee of a dozen or so men waiting for them.

'Looks like someone got across an' told 'em to expect us,' he told Yippee.

The kid jeered, 'Scared?'

'Me? I'm tremblin' all over.' But there wasn't a tremor in the big hands that gripped those reins, or in the humorous voice as he spoke.

One of the men stepped out into the roadway, his hand upraised. He was thin, black-haired under his fancy stetson, with a thin, dark moustache. He looked well-dressed, in black store clothes, and he wore light town shoes, as if he didn't ride horses much.

Careless drove smack into him. Though he saw that hand raised to halt them, he just kept driving on. The thin, dark man was so sure Careless would pull in his horses that he left it too late to get out of the way. The near-side horse shouldered into him and sent him sprawling into the dust at the feet of the other men.

Careless heard the man gasp, heard shouts from the 'reception committee', but he drove on the next fifty yards or so into the plaza, the open space in the centre of the 'dobe area. Then he shouted to his horses and stood on the brake.

Yippee screwed his head round as he saw his partner fix the brass-handled whip in the holder alongside his seat. He said quickly, 'They're comin', Careless – the hull darned lot of them.'

Careless said, 'So what?'

Then he got down, pulling his hat well down over his eyes and yawning. He started to amble across to a big building that had once been a pleasant Spanish tavern but was now a bullet-chipped saloon. He was drawing some notices out of his pocket and unfolding them.

Then the thin, dark, arrogant-looking man in dude shoes got in his way, and back of that dusty, smouldering-eyed *hombre* was the rest of the reception committee – professional gunmen if ever Careless had seen the kind.

The black-garbed man grated, 'You ran into me just then.'

The 'committee' grew threateningly closer, hands holding gun-butts. Up top the lean young Texan slipped back the safety catch of his rifle, then casually began to make another smoke.

The *hombre* snarled, 'Didn't you see I wanted you to stop?'

42

Careless said, 'I sure did.'

'Then why'n hell didn't you stop?'

'Because,' retorted Careless, 'I didn't want to stop anywhere but here, in this plaza.'

The black-garbed, town-shod man knew that this was fighting talk. It made him gasp, the audacity of the big tramp of a cowboy. Then he had another cause for gasping.

Careless had been standing there with only a big sheet of paper in his left hand. His right hand was empty. Then suddenly there was a gun in that right hand, and the thin-moustached man hadn't even seen the draw, it had been so quick.

The untidy-looking *hombre* was saying, 'Nob'dy had better draw, else this gun sure will chip chunks off your backbone, brother.' Then he called up to the lean Texan: 'Hey, kid, you jes' cover these galoots while we fix the note to the saloon door.'

The kid got excited and ripped off with a devastating, 'Yippee-ee!' And then that Henry lifted and swung up, and a dozen startled gunnies tore hands away from their gun-butts as if they'd become red-hot.

They hadn't expected it. Gunmen in numbers don't expect their victims to leap into the attack; they'd thought to intimidate this pair who had come in with the shabby old Concord, but the tables had been turned neatly upon them.

The leader of the gunnies snarled, 'I'll kill yer for this, fellar!' He knew they were being watched by the townspeople, and the neat hold-up was like bitter gall to him. Careless saw the raging fury in those brown, molten eyes and he knew the *hombre* meant it.

So the devil came into him then. Big Careless O'Connor wasn't the kind of a man to go down before a challenge. He rammed the paper into the man's hand, then fished out some nails. 'Get that stuck up on the door there, brother – pronto!'

The man looked at the bill. It read 'A coach service will operate twice a week....'

'The heck I will!' he snapped.

O'Connor lifted his Colt and let him see how big the muzzle looked from a distance of three inches. 'Changed your mind?' the big fellow asked gently.

A gasp and a stir of excitement swept round the plaza as they saw the thin man pick up a stone and hammer that bill to the unpainted, sagging door that never closed on the saloon.

Back he came to where O'Connor was standing, big and shapeless in his shabby jeans and battered hat.

He said meanly, 'I told you I'd kill you fer that. Wal, fellar, I figger you ain't gonna get outa this town alive in that caboose.'

Careless drawled, 'I figger I am.' He glanced up at Yippee. 'I figger it's time we made this stage begin ter pay, kid.'

The kid said, 'Sure, sure,' enthusiastically,

though he hadn't an idea what his boss was driving at.

So Careless switched his eyes back on to the group of gunnies and said, 'One at a time, get inside that coach. Yippee, get down while I cover 'em, then relieve 'em of their hardware as they get in.'

The kid came springing down, then gallantly kicked open a jammed door for the men to enter the coach. As they went in he pulled their Colts out from their holsters and dropped them into the dust.

That coach was made for eight people inside, but they forced all thirteen into it, though they were sitting on top of each other and swearing furiously by the time the door was slammed on them.

Careless called, 'You hang on to the doorstep, Yippee, an' see none of your passengers falls off, huh?'

Yippee got up at once, pitching his rifle on to the rack and sticking a Colt on the gunnies instead. He called, 'Where are these *hombres* goin' – boss?' And Careless didn't miss the 'boss'.

Careless got up and shook out the reins. He considered for a moment, then said, 'We c'n only take 'em into the middle of the mesa. After that I guess they'll have ter walk.'

The gunnies howled. 'The heck, we ain't gonna walk all that way back. It'll kill us!' Seven miles in riding-boots on a hot, dusty day wasn't a thing for liquor-parlour heroes to contemplate.

Young Yippee stuck that little cannon farther into the coach and said, 'Wal, ef that don't kill yer, this will.' They looked at that blue-eyed Colt and stopped arguing about a mere seven-mile walk.

The kid shouted, 'Get goin', boss. There ain't none of these passengers'll fall out while I'm here.'

Big Careless stood up on the broad footboard, and roared, 'Git a-goin', you critters!' And his whip exploded above their ears, and they plunged into their collars and the heavily laden Concord began to roll.

There was a murmur that became a mild roar as the coach swept round and then took the road out up through the 'dobe buildings, going at a smart run. It seemed the town wasn't sorry to see the gunnies humbled in this manner.

They climbed out on to the mesa. Careless kept watch all around, but after a while he relaxed and even opened up in song. It was pretty bad, and no one enjoyed it except himself.

When they were plumb in the middle of the mesa, at a water hole where the horses could slake their thirst, Careless drew rein, and dropped down into the dust.

He wasn't playing now, and his drawn Colts illustrated his mood. Yippee Clay swung down on the far side of the coach, nearly as tall as big Careless

O'Connor, and just as tough.

Careless ordered, 'Come tumblin' out – quick!'

They came out, dust-covered and running with sweat. They were as mean as a nest of rattlers.

He was brief. 'This line's got ter pay its way. Okay, you're the first passengers, and first passengers always pay high. I figger five dollars a head would be a start for the new coach company, so part up with five bucks an' look as if you enjoyed the ride.'

It was the crowning insult, but they couldn't do anything about it. When that battered, sweat-stained Stetson was held out, each in turn found five dollars.

When that was done, Careless asked a question of their leader: 'You, Laughin' Alec, tell me – what happened to Jim Whitfield, a young fellar who came in with this Concord a few day's ago?'

Laughin' Alec's thin, dark face looked meaner than ever. He said Careless O'Connor could go find out for himself!

Careless looked back along the mesa, to where a cloud of dust was growing over the trail just about where Broken Knee lay. He figured this might be pursuit, and he didn't have time to waste.

The black-garbed man spat further venom. 'Don't you ever show face in Broken Knee agen, mister. There won't be a third time fer you, ef you do!'

Careless climbed back into his seat and took up the reins before answering. From on top, though,

47

he said casually, 'This stage runs ter time, brother. It'll be in Broken Knee aroun' noon on Sat'day.' Then he leaned down and said significantly, 'When it comes in I'll look fer you, an' I'll be wantin' the answer ter my question – what happened ter Jim Whitfield in Broken Knee.'

Before the man could frame an answer, Careless' whip reeled out and sent the horses plunging away from the water hole and rearing back up to the dusty trail.

From the top of the retreating, swaying coach they looked back on the men.

The young Texan said, 'Laughin' Alec sure feels sore, boss.'

He looked at the big, untidy man beside him. He seemed quite content, placidly keeping the lead horses to the better part of the rutty trail.

After a while Burt Clay said, 'What d'you figger we made outa comin' ter Broken Knee, boss? We didn't pick up any freight, an' you bet there won't be any ter pick up while that gang runs the town.'

He slewed in his seat, then reached for his rifle. 'There's half a dozen *hombres* comin' lickety-split after us, boss,' he exclaimed urgently.

'Sure, sure,' Careless nodded. 'That ain't many. You take the reins an' give me my Sharps.'

They swopped over. The horsemen were catching up fast, strung out in a line across the broad, undulating mesa. One of the horsemen sat his mount with the reins nipped by his knee against the saddle leather and took careful aim with his rifle.

Careless knelt on his seat as the first bullet screamed overhead. Sighted as the second bullet made another hole in the back of the coach. Fired as the third bullet was about to be despatched.

And the leading rider rolled backwards off his racing pony, and that was the end of that menace.

Young Clay stood up and roared at the horses and got them racing on a down grade. They took the other slope at crazy speed and pulled over the top. The pursuers were fanning out on either side of them, creeping up slowly. No one was firing now; the tactics of those pursuers was to keep out of range and get ahead and stop the horses.

Watching narrowly, big Careless O'Connor at length said mildly, 'We'll jest keep goin' an' fight our way through.'

They did fight their way through. Suddenly the five horsemen began to converge swiftly upon the trail ahead of them, and the men on the coach realised that they were riding hell for leather in an attempt to block the way.

Careless shifted to the top of the coach. Seven shots snapped off, but though he knew he hit at least once, Careless didn't see anyone come out of the saddle – just one *hombre* pull out and ride wide, as if in pain.

Then, all at once it seemed, there were four horsemen racing level with the coach. Careless saw Colt muzzles lifting up towards him.

His Sharps was empty. He stuck it into the box,

and then, most unexpectedly, launched himself on to the nearest rider. Again it was the unexpectedness of the assault that won the day for him. Careless knocked the fellow clean out of the saddle.

The man went down into the dust, yelling dismally, then was left swiftly behind as they all raced on. The horse swerved out of line, with big Careless lying flat across its back. Then, with a sudden dextrous movement remarkable for a man of his bulk, Careless was in the saddle.

Burt saw that big flat brown face look round. Then the horse came careering in towards them, and Careless was pumping lead with Colts that hadn't been in his hands a fraction of a second before.

There was a flurry of dust rising more than horse-high, then the shock as horse ran into horse. For a few seconds there was savage fighting at close quarters, guns lifting and clubbing down.

But it wasn't Careless who pulled away from his three enemies. Watching the battle, Burt Clay saw a man tumble headlong from his saddle, saw another pull out and ride away reeling. And then the third threw in the sponge and set his horse to the tough mesquite and showed he wasn't going to fight that battle alone.

Burt yipped to his horses and stood on his heels and leaned his full weight against the reins to get the coach under control again. When they were down to walking pace he looked back and saw that

Careless was sitting his horse across the trail, as if to dare the enemy to come riding along it again. But the enemy had had enough.

Careless came galloping up. The younger man grinned down and called, 'You sure did upset that bunch o' rattlers, boss!'

Now it was boss all the time. Since the trouble in Broken Knee the younger man certainly had changed in his attitude towards Careless O'Connor.

FOUR

THE DEPUTATION!

They halted on the outskirts of Neuces Bend.
Careless said he was going to drive the coach into
the cattle town, and the horse could run behind.
They tied his newly-acquired horse to the coach,
then Careless got up and took the reins from Burt
and started the horses down the main street.

A startled town saw the battered, trail-dusty old
Concord come in at a spanking pace, two six-foot
Texans lounging comfortably high up on the seat.
Word went round like lightning— 'The stage is
back!' And at that everyone turned out to welcome
it, for no one had thought to see it again.

A flood of people came flocking round, so that
for a moment they were unable to descend. Grace
struggled through and climbed halfway up to
them. Careless held out his hand and she gripped
it and smiled a welcome to him. 'Oh, Careless,

53

we've been worrying so. I'm glad you didn't run into any trouble!'

Careless heard young Burt Clay gasp at that, but he didn't turn round. Instead he said, quite steadily, 'It sure was a good job we didn't run into trouble – much.'

Grace asked, 'Did you get any business?'

'Business?' Careless sat back as if to consider. 'Sure, we brought a dozen passengers out to the mesa water hole.'

'Thirteen,' corrected Yippee.

'They paid us five dollars a time. I reckon we're showin' a profit already, Gracie,' Careless said.

There was a gasp of amazement at that from the crowd. 'You picked up passengers in Broken Knee?' The questioner's voice was incredulous. 'What'n tarnation do fellars want ter ride out ter that water hole for? An' how're they gonna get back?'

Careless started to climb down, and said, 'Brother, that's one thing we don't do on this hyar line. We never ask our customers their business.'

No mention was made to anyone – not even to Gracie – of the shindig they'd had in Broken Knee and along the trail, and Burt Clay was quick to see through O'Connor's tactics.

For as they were drifting away, the crowd was saying, 'Ef they're lettin' the coach run into Broken Knee, then thar's no reason why we shouldn't use it.'

True, no one came forward to book a place as a

passenger, but there were lots of packages people said they wanted delivering to friends, relatives and business acquaintances across the mesa.

Sitting with his boots off to air his feet on the back porch of the Wrigleys', Careless said complacently, to young Yippee, 'I figger there's plenty business a-tween here an' Broken Knee, brother.'

The lean, brown-faced young puncher looked cautiously around, then said, 'I figger there's plenty trouble, too, Careless – heap plenty trouble. They'll be waitin' for us next time. You know that?'

Careless wriggled his toes. 'That's how I want it.'

Then Grace came out to say there was food waiting for them. Careless reached for his tattered boots. Then the effort to stoop and pull them on was too much for him, and he padded inside on feet big enough to hold up a grizzly. As they went in, Grace managed to ask a question.

'Jim?' She looked strained and anxious.

Careless admitted, 'I didn't find out fer you, Gracie. We had ter turn round right away, because of our passengers. But there's a fellar will have news fer me when I go in on Sat'day.'

'Did he promise?'

'He'll have it,' was all that Careless said reassuringly.

As they took their place at the table, Cathy saw the big fellow's bare feet. She also saw that Grace was frowning at them, as if she didn't approve. When Grace went out for more rye bread, Cathy spoke up.

'You want to watch out, Careless. Grace is threatening to take you in hand and smarten you up. And I'll bet she doesn't let you come to the table again without boots, you see!'

'Aw, heck.' The big man's tone was full of disgust. 'I like it this way. Why doesn't she leave me alone?'

Later that night, when the lamp was lit in the store for any late customers, Ben found the big fellow fixing his shirt with a pair of pliers and some fence wire. He was growling. 'Doggone it, I don' like buttons. I ain't gonna have buttons. Buttons is allus comin' off.'

Ben want back into the living-room behind the shop. He had hardly settled into a chair when he heard a mutter of voices from inside the shop. He looked at his wife, then tilted back in his chair so as to see inside the store.

Careless was standing right under the lamp, facing the black void of the street through the open door. He was crouching, his hands on his gun butts, as if he was threatened by danger.

Ben sent his chair legs crashing to the ground, then, all in the same movement went reeling back towards the store. As he came in, Careless held up his hand, as if to keep him back, and Ben stood irresolute in the doorway.

He heard Careless say softly to someone out beyond in the darkness, 'I'm comin' out, fellar. Let's see ef your promises are good.'

He hefted a gun, then gestured for Ben to stay

where he was, and went padding on his bare feet out on to the unpaved street.

Ben waited, expecting every moment to hear a burst of gunfire, but none came. After a while he went back to his seat. He felt uneasy – at times like this he always remembered that rumour made big Careless O'Connor to be a renegade. And one of the voices outside had sounded Mexican to him.

The whispered voice had stolen on Careless' ears as he sat finishing off the wiring in place of buttons on his faded shirt. Just a voice that said, 'O'Connor?'

He had turned at once, facing through the open door into the dark street. He didn't speak.

Then again that voice came to him – 'You don't need ter be skeered, O' Connor. We ain't plannin' no harm on yer.' It was an oldish voice, harsh as most men's voices were out there, and it still didn't inspire confidence.

Careless rested his hand on a gun butt. 'Why don't you come in where there's light, then?' he challenged. Ben came to the door just after that.

Another voice interrupted. 'Because we don't want to be seen talking to you, amigo.' And this voice wasn't Texan; there was a rich, liquid Spanish sound about the vowels.

Acting on a hunch, Careless started to walk forward, drawing his gun at the same time, nevertheless. That first, rough old voice growled, 'You c'n put away that toothpick, O'Connor. Ef we'd bin that way inclined, we c'd have shot you in the back while you was prettyin' that shirt of yours.'

Careless knew that was true, and he holstered his four-five and went padding silently forward to where the speaker was. As he moved into the darkness, his eyes began to adjust to the decrease in light and he saw three men standing there, backs against the wall.

He asked softly, 'You from Broken Knee?'

The voice growled again, 'How d'you guess?' Then, rather urgently, 'Come a piece up the street with us, O'Connor. We've got a proposition for you.'

Careless said, 'Okay,' but under cover of the darkness he drew his guns again.

He ambled along with the men, taking care to keep a few yards behind their shadowy figures. The sandy soil was still warm to his feet, following the long soaking with sunshine that day. He liked the feel of it. They stopped, near to where a fourth man held some horses right at the end of the new street of clapboard buildings.

The gruff voice said, 'You don't need ter know who we are, O'Connor, 'cept that we're friends. All I'll tell yer is that we're a depitation to yer from Broken Knee. We four are jes' people who live in an' around the town, farmin', tradin' – and jes' workin'.'

Careless asked softly, 'What's all the mystery about? Why didn't you come in ter see me, like honest men?'

'After what you did today,' was the grim rejoinder, 'we wouldn't live long, ef we was seen talkin' ter Careless O'Connor. An' we figger there's always someone in all these Border towns ready to take news of that kind inter Broken Knee.'

Careless felt at ease now and silently holstered his guns again. Now he knew these men were friends.

Careless said, 'Now tell me what it's all about.'

'About six months ago, things began ter happen in Broken Knee,' the old-sounding man said. 'There's a fellar got a bit of land in the Bottom-lands by Winter's Bridge. He don't do much with it – jes' runs a few longhorns an' lets the place go wild.'

Careless slowly stiffened. The voice went on speaking, but Careless was listening for other sounds.

'I'm talkin' about the Big Mouth, a fellar called David Simms. He's as big as you are, but soft with it, an' he never stops mouthin'. He was driven out at the beginnin' of the war with Mexico, an' now he's back he hates everythin' Spanish or Mexican. Don't he, Carlos, amigo—' He stopped abruptly, as if inadvertently he had said too much.

The Spanish sounding voice laughed from the darkness, tolerantly. 'Okay, Joseph. I guess Senor O'Connor will be safe with my identity.' And then, in a different tone, grimly, he said, 'But it is true. He would have my land because I am an original Spanish ranchero, only my good friends have stood by me against him.'

'Yeah – but we can't hold him back much longer,' growled the old man. Careless was watching a shadow, faintly discernible against the softer blackness of the night sky. That was why he had squatted; from that position in the dark a man could see a little better than if he were standing.

'The Big Mouth's up ter somethin' – an' he's gettin' big. Every few weeks men come ridin' in from all parts of the county, an' they're the toughest *hombres* you'll find anywhere along the Border.

Careless interposed – 'How many?' – watching that shadow.

There was a pause for reflection, then the old man said, 'I figger as many as a hundred men gather together at those times. They gather together over two or three days, then all in one night there's not a one of them to be seen out at Simms' Running S ranch. The Big Mouth, he doesn't show up, either, not for a week or two.'

'The boss goes with the men, huh? A hundred men?' Careless whistled softly. Another shadow had joined the first.

'Sure. We don't know what they're up to—' It was the old man speaking again. 'All we know is suddenly the men are all back again, flush with money, an' for a few days they drink an' gamble an' turn Broken Knee into a hell on earth for quieter citizens. Then they all vamoose, an' everythin's quiet fer another two or three weeks.'

'They're gathering now, aren't they?' Careless

saw another shadow down away from the town. Shadows on the mesa, he was thinking, and he knew what they were. But he wanted to hear the finish of this story, and he thought there was still time.

'Yeah, they've bin ridin' in since yesterday. The Big Mouth's runnin' the town through Fergie Allbright.' Hatred exploded in that old voice as he mentioned the two names. 'When all this started, Fergie got together the worst crooks an' card-sharps an' men on the run – an' we've got plenty, mister, I c'n tell you – an' he's bin usin' 'em ter run the town.'

'We raised an objection when we saw the sweepin's o' the Border driftin' in an' shootin' up the town periodically, but Fergie jes' came at us with his gang an' shot the objection out of us.'

The third man spoke for the first time. A younger man, this time. 'I figger Fergie makes so much money outa them sprees that he intends ter fight ef there are attempts to keep the Border scum outa the town.'

Careless was rising to his feet, his eyes on that patch of crawling shadow. 'Couldn't be that Fergie an' the Big Mouth are in cahoots on something, huh? It might be a deep game. Fergie might be indispensable to the Big Mouth. You say David Simms hates Mexes....' The men didn't understand him. Careless uttered another sentence, and they didn't understand that, either.

'Ef a fellar gets his pocket emptied quick, he's

61

gotta come back soon ter fill it again, huh?'

His voice became brisker, more purposeful. He knew he had only a few seconds left. 'Why come all this way ter tell me that?'

'Because,' said a desperate voice, that of the old man, 'we're tired of bein' terrorised by Border scum. We're helpless, we citizens of Broken Knee. We know that ef we do anythin' agen the Big Mouth or Fergie or any of their followers, we jes' don't live.'

'So you look to someone outside to help you?'

'Yeah. An' when we saw what you did ter Fergie an' his pards, we figgered you was just the man ter organise somethin' agen them varmints. Can you help clean out the pocket o' vipers, O'Connor?'

'Mebbe. First thing, though, is fer you fellars ter find out what game the Big Mouth's up to. I've been wantin' ter know fer weeks now,' he said, but again that was something that didn't add up in their consciousness.

Then he told them to go. It startled them, what he told them. They heard his voice come softly to them out of the darkness and they realised that the big man was stealing silently away.

'Time you went, fellars, we got visitors. I aim ter find out who it is who's sneakin' in on us. Keep talkin' a coupla minutes, then they won't notice me creepin' up. Then get your hosses an' hightail it outa here. Mebbe this place ain't gonna be so healthy next hour or so.'

The last they heard of Careless that night was a

whisper from the darkness— 'I'll come across when I can ... will seek out Carlos. We'll do some plannin' then....'

A minute later he heard the men go across and mount their horses. There was a jingle of metal and a creak of stretching leather, and then hoofs pad-padded softly through the dust.

Almost at the same instant something touched his bare foot. It was a warm hand. Careless was waiting for that moment, and his hand went down and gripped. Something fell off into the darkness, and that told Careless who the enemy were.

Now he acted like lightning. His hands relaxed on that gasping throat, and instead one mighty arm crooked about it, just as effectually choking the man. Careless' weight crushed his victim to the dust. He felt muscles bunching and fighting frantically under the bare skin, but in that powerful grip the man in the shadow hadn't a chance.

Careless saw the rush of other fleet-footed shadows towards him, caught the curving arc of glistening steel. A Colt jumped into his right hand, and the night's silence was shattered by the explosion as the first round blasted off.

Instantly there was pandemonium. All around nearly naked men came rushing from the shadows; then horsemen went plunging towards the light along the straggling main street.

Careless let go of his victim, grabbed the sombrero that had fallen in the dust, and ran back towards the store. His gun stabbed flame from the darkness, but when a returning volley smashed back he wasn't where he had been a second before.

The town was in an uproar. Men were tumbling out from the saloon and from the houses and other establishments. They came with their rifles ready, because it sounded like an Indian attack, all this screaming and shooting. Then they saw the first of the Mexicans riding furiously down the centre of the street.

They went firing indiscriminately as they rode their hardy little Border ponies through the patches of yellow lamplight. The citizens of Neuces Bend saw moustaches, sallow faces, excited glittering eyes – saw the lust for murder, plunder and revenge on the faces of these men who should now be at peace with their country, according to the politicians of both sides.

The Mexicans were pouring into the town, seemingly in hundreds. A building began to burn, and instantly the place was lit up with a leaping yellow glow.

A mass of Mexican horsemen, their bodies glistening in the wild, orange light, came crowding up to Wrigley's store, intent on battering down the door and getting inside. Ben was shooting steadily through a crack in the door and for the moment was holding them back. Someone else started shooting from the hastily barricaded window, and Careless guessed it would be Yippee

Clay. The girls, like true frontiers women, would be down on the floor, reloading spare weapons, he knew.

A door crashed in along the street and a dozen Mexicans leapt from their horses and went inside. There was vicious hand-to-hand fighting inside. Careless, hard back in the shadows, saw men stagger out and fall and then creep away like dogs that have been hurt as much as they can stand.

Another building began to burn, and then another. It was like the early Border war all over again.

Careless couldn't get into any of the buildings, so he clung to the shadows and hoped to escape in the general turmoil.

To aid him, he put on the sombrero, and then he caught a riderless horse and went plunging down the street with the rest of the marauders. When he came out beyond the fire, where the shadows were the darker because of it, he wheeled and opened up again with his Colts.

Probably because he had managed to give a few seconds' warning, the attack on the town was an expensive failure from the first. If the lithe Mexicans could have got into the houses before the doors were bolted and the barricades were up at the windows, the result would have been a massacre of the white settlers.

Protected within their dwellings, and with newer, more accurate weapons than those of the

Mexicans, the citizens of Neuces Bend were on top within minutes of the alarm being sounded. The Mexicans fought viciously, bravely, for a while longer in the teeth of that deadly fire, and then they began to pull out beyond the leaping light from those blazing buildings.

Someone among the settlers took charge. Men were sent out to act as scouts, to make sure that the Mexicans had really retreated. They met Careless O'Connor riding in along the trail. He was still barefooted, but was now without sombrero.

He called out, 'You don't need ter worry, fellars. Them Mexes is hightailin' it for the Border.'

In the darkness he saw them gather together and mutter among themselves, then a couple of them raced along the trail as if they wanted to make sure for themselves.

The others fell in behind O'Connor as he rode back into the town. Other citizens were out now, throwing water on to buildings adjoining those that were still burning furiously. Someone said something as O'Connor came ambling up on his bare backed pony, and at that they all turned and looked at him. He saw that Ben was among them, and Ben turned away when he saw him.

Then a man came stumbling forward, a big tree of a man, as solid as Careless on top, but thicker and heavier down below. Careless, startled, looked into a face that was black with passion.

Then the man roared, 'You darned renegade!' And tried to smash O'Connor out of the saddle.

FIVE

A SECRET SHARED!

Careless just saw the blow in time and rolled so that the force was spent before the huge fist caught him on the shoulder. In the same movement he slid out of his saddle, and came ducking under his horse's head to face the settler. He remembered seeing him in the town the previous day, and thought that the man's name was Leach or Geach … that was it, Daniel Geach.

As soon as Geach saw him he flung himself on to Careless in utter fury. He was like an enraged dog, shouting while he hammered, all his limbs working in a fury of motion.

Men were running up, shouting – and the encouragement was for Geach. Within seconds there was a jostling, milling mob around the contestants, a fiercely angry crowd who lifted savage roaring voices in a din of approval – of Geach's attack.

Geach came battering in at his head, and Careless crouched and took shelter behind his uplifted arms. Then suddenly he came springing forward, gripping Geach round the neck and hipping him. Geach went rolling into the dust.

The shouts from the crowd rose higher at that, as if in frustration; the note of savagery was intensified. And above the noise one word kept coming through clearly – 'Renegade!'

Geach got on to his knees, panting, his eyes murderous as they alighted on Careless. Then he lurched forward, hairy fists trying to break through Careless' defence. But Careless fought on the retreat, shuffling backwards and sideways, ducking and weaving, twisting and dodging. Then suddenly in he came again and grabbed Geach and wrestled with him.

Careless heard him gasp, 'Damn renegade … bringin' Mexes … killed … my brother!'

Careless threw him yet again, and he lay on his back for seconds, feebly stirring, trying to get his wind back into that heaving, barrel-like chest.

Then there was a rush from other incensed men, and Careless found himself being charged by a crowd. He had three men sprawling in the dust before they knew what had hit them. He slammed out at another man, but then they were flooding on top of him.

He was helpless when finally they rolled away

and dragged him to his feet; someone got a rope round him, and after that struggle was useless. The mob dragged him towards the light of a burning building, and the cry was already going up, that cry of the savage mob – 'String him up! Lynch him!'

Then Grace was there, right in front of them, terrified of the mob but braving it to try to help the man who had done so much for her. And with her was Cathy, darker, not so vividly handsome – Cathy, that fine, courageous frontierswoman.

But Ben wasn't with them. Careless noticed that right away.

The mob just kept marching on, pushing the helpless prisoner against the girls. Above the roaring of the men around him, Careless could hear the girls appealing for his life.

At the same moment a man stepped forward, barring the way to the gallows tree. He was lean and lithe and six-foot of young Texas manhood, and he carried a brace of Colts in his hands.

It was Burt Clay, cowpuncher turned stagecoach guard. Yippee Clay, only he wasn't yippeeing at the moment.

The crowd came to a halt, the prisoner to the fore, the girls clinging to him in their frantic efforts to delay mob justice. The roaring died to a murmur. And when he could be heard, that young Texan spoke. His voice crackled with icy contempt.

'You goldarned sheep,' he said. 'This fellar ain't no renegade. Let go of him!'

But the crowd wouldn't. Instead the murmur

went swelling up into a roar of fury that now included Burt Clay.

Burt Clay was crouching, shouting his lungs out so that they could hear his challenge.

'You're not gonna hang O'Connor. I ain't gonna let you. I'll fight you one at a time, O'Connor to go free ef I win!'

A vain challenge; mobs didn't listen to such talk.

Then Burt came jumping forward in a desperate attempt to free his boss. He crashed right in among the group who held Careless a prisoner. His guns belched flame and noise, but he fired just across the faces of the nearest men, so that the bullets did no harm. It sent them pulling back in fear, however, and when they felt those gun barrels slamming into their stomachs they got their hands off Careless pretty quickly.

As soon as the grip slackened on his shoulders, big Careless went jumping forward without having to be told what to do. Grace and Cathy ran after him, eager hands seeking to get the ropes off him. Young Clay jumped back, then standing in front of the little group, protecting them.

Careless, struggling out of the ropes, heard young Clay shouting defiance at the mob. He was daring them to come on – telling them what he would do if they did.

A savage howl went up when it was seen that the big man was free. The crowd expected to see him break away and run and seek escape in the near darkness. Only, Careless didn't run for it.

Instead, he padded back on his bare feet straight up to the crowd, and that was the last thing they expected.

Even in the tatters of his shirt that gaped to reveal his mighty, hairy chest; even with the swellings and cuts on his face following the brawl – he was somehow a commanding presence. And when he lifted both hands into the air in a sign for silence, it was curious but it came instantly.

His deep, massive voice floated easily to the ears even of the farthermost audience. 'Friends,' he called, 'just now I've heard myself called renegade. Wal, I'm no renegade, an' I aim ter stop here an' talk agen anyone who says I am.' His voice ended on a fiercely challenging note.

'The hell, didn't we see you ridin' with the Mexes – wearin' a sombrero?' roared Geach irately. He was working himself up into a murderous, hating rage again.

Big Careless flung his hand out in derision. 'How long d'you think I'd have lived among them Mexes ef I hadn't worn a sombrero?' He faced the crowd more directly, and spoke to them over the head of the thick-set, lowering Geach.

'I was caught out there when the Mexes charged in. But I gave you warnin' – thank me fer that. Ef I hadn't been outside they'd have shot the town up afore anyone could have got up ter barricade a door. I caught one o' their scouts an' picked up his sombrero, then got on a Mexican hoss because I was right in the middle of 'em an' that was the only

73

way I could think of to escape.'

Someone jeered, 'Yeah, it all totes up nicely, don't it, O'Connor? Now you tell us what you was doin' out beyond the town at this time o' night. Meetin' up with your Mex friends, huh?'

'I was out along the street talkin' ter friends,' he shouted.

'Creepin' around without boots?' yelled back the voice from the crowd.

'When your feet are as big as mine,' rapped O'Connor, 'you're always glad ter get out of your boots, brother!'

That little note of humour more than anything swayed the crowd away from their dangerous mood now.

'What you fellars want ter ask yourself,' Careless shouted, 'is – why did the Mexes come all this way across the Border to attack Neuces Bend? That's somethin' you want ter figger out!'

He put a question into their minds, and the moment a mob begins to think it ceases to become a mob and becomes instead just a lot of people.

So Careless went on talking, winning them over to his side.

'If I was in cahoots with the Mexes, would I show myself with 'em when they rode into town, then ride back right into your arms? Talk sense, fellars. A guy must be crazy to behave like that.

'No, I came back because there was nothin' on my conscience. An' I did my bit in the fightin' agen them Mexes,' he went on grimly. 'Now, the thing that's in my mind is this – why did they come here at all? Why Neuces Bend an' not some other place? Why set the Border alight, anyway, when our two countries are at peace with each other?'

He looked at the buildings, now burning out – looked at the bodies that lay in the dust, Mexican and Texan side by side. His face was grim. He'd seen too much of war in recent years and wanted an end to it.

Abruptly he called to Burt. 'You c'n put away them shootin' irons, Yippee. They won't be needed now.'

He caught Grace by the hand and began to walk across to the Wrigley store. There was a murmur from the crowd at that.

So big Careless O'Connor halted and faced them toughly. 'Ef you want me,' he snapped, 'I'll be aroun' termorrow ter finish this discussion. I figger you folks'd best be lookin' to your houses, 'stead of botherin' about me.'

There was significance in his remark, because a gust of wind was eddying sparks around and some were settling once again on the adjacent buildings and they weren't going out.

Cathy ran up and caught his arm on the other side and began to tow the big man towards her home. The crowd muttered, then young Burt Clay came striding up behind, his hands resting on his gun butts.

Careless growled, 'I sure got me a friend in that young hellion. I never expected it – right until a little time ago he sure seemed ter hate my guts.'

Cathy laughed, 'Don't you know why, Careless? Ever since you beat up the Broken Knee gunnies he's done nothing but talk about you.' She squeezed his arm. 'Don't you understand, Careless? This is hero worship. You can't do anything wrong with Burt after that.'

Then they came to the Wrigleys' place. Ben had gone back and relit the lamp, and now he was standing in the open doorway, rifle in hand.

He growled, 'Stay where you are, O'Connor. You don't come in my house agen.'

They all stopped, astonished. Careless asked, softly, 'What's bitin', Ben?'

Ben didn't answer. Cathy asked, bewildered, 'Ben, what do you mean by that? Didn't you hear what Careless told the crowd?'

Her husband said grimly, 'I did, an' I don't believe a word of it.'

'Ben!' Cathy tried to catch hold of him, to restrain his words, but Ben pushed her away, filled as he was with righteous indignation.

'I'll say what I intend ter say ter this renegade,' he snarled. 'I heard him talk ter that crowd, an' I knew it was lies. He sure can put axle grease on his words, this *hombre*, but he won't take me in no more.' Deliberately he said, 'Ef I had opened my mouth, I c'd have put the noose right back round his thick neck – where it should be.'

Big Careless pushed the two girls away and stood in front of the raging man. He spoke, even in the face of that affront, without heat.

'What d'you mean, Ben – you could have put the noose on me ef you'd opened your mouth? Come, man, talk up an' let's get this thing settled.'

'The crowd forgot ter ask you who those friends were you were talkin' with when the raid started. They were the Mexes, come ter warn yer ter keep outa the way when the trouble started. Your good amigos, weren't they, O'Connor?' His voice was bitter.

Careless sighed. Now he understood. Carlos had spoken to him from the darkness, Carlos from Broken Knee, with his Spanish voice. Ben thought that voice to belong to a Mexican.

Cathy took her husband's arm, and her head was shaking obstinately. 'Ben, you're making a mistake. I don't care what you think – I'm certain Careless is straight and can explain.'

They waited in silence then, waited for Careless to tell them the truth of what had happened. But he just couldn't say anything, without betraying the confidence of that deputation from Broken Knee; if he spoke he endangered their lives, for if word got about and their identity was suspected, by all accounts the Big Mouth's gang wouldn't be merciful to them.

When he couldn't stand the silence any longer, Careless said, 'Mebbe Burt'll fetch my boots afore mornin'. I'm turnin' in now.' And with that he swung round and walked slowly into the darkness.

He left four chilled and silent friends. Burt

collected the worn old boots and followed after Careless to the old Concord. When he looked inside Burt found it was empty.

Then Careless hailed him softly from under a built-up frame house. He'd got down there with his blanket and was curled up ready for sleep.

Careless drawled good-humouredly, 'I figgered so many people still kinda feel doubtful about me, mebbe I'd have visitors tonight ef I slept agen in that old coach.'

Burt squatted miserably by his side. He said mournfully, 'I don't want ter think what I'm thinkin' now, Careless. You're a big, ugly slob of a no-good, but I kinda got ter like you, an' – aw, heck, tell a fellow ef there's any truth in this renegade story!' he ended desperately.

But Careless just said, 'Wal, Burt, I ain't no renegade, but there's a lot I jes' can't talk about right now.'

Eagerly Burt exclaimed, 'I won't open my mouth, Careless. You c'n tell me anythin'.'

But big Careless just settled back in his blanket and said comfortably, 'A secret shared ain't no secret any longer.' And then went to sleep. When he awoke it was to find Burt Clay rolled in his blanket only a couple of yards away. Burt had made up his mind. He'd decided that Careless was all right, and he was going to stick by him, with or without explanations.

And that night Burt had slept with his Colt under his hand, ready to use it if anyone tried to jump the sleeping man in the dark.

There wasn't a deal of friendliness shown towards Careless O'Connor next day on the part of the tired citizens of Neuces Bend. All the same, there was no direct affront given to the big stage-line driver when he went about the town, drumming up business.

The first apparently uneventful trip to and from Broken Knee had encouraged the Neuces Bend citizens to use the stage line. True there was no one brave enough to book a place as a passenger, but there was plenty of freight to take over.

That Friday night, just about the time a man had had enough drink to make his tongue wag, Careless began to notice a change in attitude towards him. The people were getting more friendly.

Then he began to realise that the secret was out, that Neuces Bend knew of the trouble they'd had on that first trip to the neighbouring town. Someone had been talking hard in his favour, and he felt he knew who it was.

He went round the saloon, pushing his way through the throng until he found him.

The kid was sprawling across a table right back of the room. Big Careless took a handful of thick black hair and lifted his head for him. At that Burt opened eyes that were rimmed with misery, but his smile was gallant as he saw this boss that he'd started to worship.

' 'Lo, boss,' he slurred. His youthful face was

flushed, and his eyes were heavy, as if he could hardly keep them open. He grinned, 'I had ter go get myself cock-eyed, boss. Reckon I've felt as bad today as I've ever felt.'

Careless patted him on the shoulder, but all he said was, 'Now you understand why I can't share secrets with you, son?'

'For fear I go get stinko an' open my mouth?' Careless nodded. Burt sighed wearily and drooped forward. His tired voice continued – 'Mebbe you're right. But mebbe you're wrong, boss. Mebbe ef I knew … fer sure … I wouldn't need the darn' bottle. I did it ter make fellars think well of you. I don't know anyone I like better than you.'

But Careless knew. Just by the batwings he murmured, 'I know someone – Gracie. That's why you're so fed up tonight, Burt, ain't it?'

The kid sighed. 'You're right, boss. I reckon I've never known a gal like Gracie, an' I'm breakin' my heart because I know she never even sees me when you're around.'

And Careless just said, softly as ever, 'Mebbe you're right, Burt, but mebbe you c'n change her mind for her.'

He shoved out through the batwings, helping the lean young Texan with him. The light from the saloon showed them up as tall silhouettes. Careless heard one word from the blackness, just as the batwings began to close behind him.

One word – 'Right!'

He kicked Burt's legs from under him and

crashed down on to the ground against the saloon wall.

There was a gunshot blast from the darkness opposite the saloon. It sounded as loud as a cannon, and the red flame from the muzzle tuliped out to a size that told the prostrate O'Connor that the barrel of the shotgun had been sawn off.

SIX

DYNAMITE!

Only the nearness of the hidden enemy saved his life. A few yards farther back, and the wide-spreading blast of shot must surely have hit him. As it was it smashed holes in the flimsy batwing doors and hurled them back on their hinges.

Careless rolled a few yards, then crashed off with both guns as he caught a movement in the shadows of a 'dobe dwelling just along from him.

Then he heard the rattle of hoofs on stone and some horses – he thought three in number – went racing away through the old Spanish town. Back of him, the saloon was silent, every man there holding his breath, wanting to know what was going on outside.

Then the door swung open. Big Careless O'Connor came edging in. He was carrying his employee, Burt Clay, and Burt had taken a few stray pellets in his shoulder, but it was that unexpected throw to the ground that had put him out of consciousness.

Careless jerkily explained as he tried to revive the kid. 'I went out – heard someone shout ''Right!'' – an' at once I got the feelin' someone was tryin' ter dry-gulch me.'

'Some friend from Broken Knee?' queried one of the men, remembering the story that the young Texan had given out.

Careless nodded. He was relieved to see that young Clay was coming round. 'I threw young Yippee down, then dropped myself. I wasn't takin' chances. I reckon Yippee musta hit his head.'

They got the half-conscious Texan to his bed, where he promptly and wisely fell fast asleep again. And again Careless didn't sleep in the old Concord. Neither did he sleep underneath the frame building, where he'd slept the previous night.

He had plenty of enemies around him, and like the deer on the plains he preferred a new bed every night.

Promptly on time next morning he brought the battered old coach up to the door of the hardware store run by the Wrigleys. Ben didn't show up. Evidently he was nursing his distrust of his former friend.

But Cathy was there, looking a little pale and strained, as if she didn't like being his friend when her husband was his enemy.

And Grace was there, too, looking young and very lovely. She was concerned, worrying for him, and her face was flushed and her eyes were sparkling bright.

People came crowding up, standing against the tall wheels, and they were all talking to him.

'You don't want ter go, Careless.'

'Why stick your neck out in Broken Knee?'

'You'll run slap bang into a bigger bit o' dry-gulchin' than last night's bungle.'

When Grace heard the warnings she became even nearer to tears. 'Oh, Careless, don't go! They'll kill you, and – and I shall blame myself for it always! This time you haven't even got Yippee to hold a gun for you. It's madness, going in alone!'

Careless was getting uncomfortable at all this advice and shook out the reins. 'Burt ain't fit enough ter ride, an' I told him so. But I'll get along fine without him. Now I'm goin', an' I won't come back without news of your brother, Grace. Adios!'

He whipped up the horses into good speed, taking the old box on wheels at a spanking pace out of the town. He came up out of the dip at the end of the street, just beyond where he'd first seen the Mexican raiders, and saw two men sitting their horses at the side of the trail.

They had rifles and both waved as the lumbering coach came swaying over the little hill that gave out on to the mesa. One signalled to him to stop, and at once Careless stood up and roared at his horses and pulled on the reins. He braked, and the wheels locked and skidded and made long tracks in the hot, sun-drenched dust, and then they were halted, and the men were walking across.

One asked, 'You take passengers ter Broken Knee, brother?'

Careless considered. 'Could do, I reckon, ef you ride on top,' he told them.

'That's where we aimed ter travel in the first place,' said Burt Clay, and came up the side of the coach one-handed, his left arm being in a sling. 'Our horses will natcherally go home!'

The other man followed and sat down without saying a word or even so much as looking at Careless on the driving seat. He had the grim, angry look of a man caught out in an unexpected weakness. And that's how Ben Wrigley felt at that moment.

Careless yelled to the horses and got them into movement again, and they travelled under the broiling sun across the bleached and deserted mesa for some time before he spoke.

Then he jerked out of the corner of his mouth: 'Thought I told you to stay off this run today, Burt?' His face was expressionless as his narrowed eyes followed the trail ahead.

'Sure,' agreed Burt. 'I heard you, too. But I figgered you didn't oughta go into Broken Knee alone, so – wal, here I am.'

'And why are you ridin' with me now, Ben?' asked Careless.

It made Ben think for an answer, and when it came it was mumbled and not too clear.

'They've all bin at me, sayin' you shouldn't ride alone. Grace, Burt an' even my own wife. I got so I couldn't listen no more to 'em, so I told Burt I'd come along.'

That's all he said, but it was enough for Careless. He knew that after all Ben was having doubts about him and his conscience was sending him on this journey just in case the new doubts were right.

They halted at the water hole and let their four horses have their fill, then they resumed their journey on to Broken Knee.

When they were a couple of miles from the town, just where the trail dipped into a hollow that was well-clothed with thorn scrub, they saw a man rise from some shade by a thick patch, pull out a horse from the cover, mount and go hurtling ahead of them into Broken Knee.

Burt said: 'That fellar's hightailed it into town ter make sure there's a reception committee for us.'

Which was what Careless wanted, anyway.

Yet when they came down the sloping street that led into the plaza, at first there was no sign of an enemy.

Careless came driving in at a spanking pace, so as to impress the local people. He wheeled and came to a halt in front of the 'dobe cantina, skidding the wheels and roaring at the top of his voice.

But nothing happened. No gunnies showed up,

so the people came out a little way into the hot sunshine. Careless saw the movement and encouraged it by reading out a name on a parcel. He shouted it out and held it up, then picked up a second parcel and shouted the name of the addressee on that, too.

A man who hadn't bothered to tie up his boots came shambling eagerly across. When the crowd saw him go away with his parcel, they forgot their caution and came pressing round the coach to see if any mail or parcels had come for them. There was quite a lot, and it took some time to distribute the mail and freight to the jostling, calling, pleasantly excited crowd.

Then people began to stream back with freight that was wanted in Neuces Bend; some of it was fulfilment of orders that Careless had brought with him, and it was clear there was quite a little business to be developed between the two towns.

But at last it was time for Careless to drive away. He'd got down, when he was sure there was no enemy in the crowd that surrounded the coach, so that it stood out like a little island in a sea of bobbing heads. He was about to clamber back when he heard a familiar voice say, 'We wanna see you tonight, O'Connor. Meet us at the water hole after dark. It's urgent.' And there was a note of urgency in the man's voice.

Careless shouted to the people to clear a way, then bellowed at his horses and swung the whip crackling over their ears. They went pulling across the plaza, with quite a lot of good wishes coming after them.

And then Careless stood on the brake and leaned back on the long reins and brought the coach to a slithering halt.

Four men had suddenly walked into the street ahead, blocking it; they had Colts out, in their hands, and their hard-faced, grim-eyed appearance said they were more than eager to use them.

Fergie Allbright, the gambling man, was there in the midst of them, and his face registered the ugly triumph of his soul. Careless looked down at him, and adjusted a rope behind his seat. One end was tied to the rail on top of the coach.

Careless settled comfortably in his seat, then Burt heard him say, 'Fix yourself a cigarette, Yippee. We'll soon be needin' it.'

Burt didn't understand, but with his one good hand he began to roll himself a curly. What the boss said went with young Burt Clay.

Fergie Allbright came nearer, and with him his men. Thin, black-garbed Fergie was quite sure that this time Careless O'Connor was in his power. The one thing that worried the gambling man was that the big, sprawling, weather-beaten man on the box didn't seem to show the slightest apprehension.

Careless brought the gunnies' wrath to the boil by asking, casually: 'You fellars opine ter ride out ter that water hole agen?'

Burt had rolled his curly and was putting it in his mouth.

Allbright snarled up, 'You ain't gonna get away with what you did, big ape! Nor your friends. You killed one o' my men—'

'I didn't start the fight.' Careless was sprawling so far back now that he almost looked to be lying down. He was taking things very much at ease; even Burt Clay and Ben Wrigley couldn't make him out.

'Yeah,' snarled Allbright. 'You c'n get down from off that seat, you big ox, you an' your friends. You ain't goin' anywhere but a li'l piece along a road outa Broken Knee – an' this time you're gonna do the walkin', see?'

Careless said mildly, 'I ain't got feet that like walkin', brother. Sides, I opine ter get this coach through ter Neuces Bend within the next coupla hours or so.'

One of the gunnies shouted: 'Quit talkin' ter him, Fergie. Let's give him his now!'

At that the other men began to growl and come lurching forward threateningly. It was the critical moment, and all three on top of the coach knew it.

Burt's match spluttered and he held it to his cigarette. It was as good a cigarette as he'd ever made, in spite of the tension and the fact that he didn't need this particular curly. He felt a movement against him – big Careless shoved the end of a paper-wrapped parcel into the match flame.

Instantly something spluttered acridly into Yippee's face, and he drew back with a startled yell.

Then the parcel was neatly flicked down to the feet of the advancing group. They saw spluttering smoke, smelled saltpetre burning. And instantly big Careless bellowed at the top of his lungs: 'Dynamite! A powerful present fer you, you sons-of-no-good cowhands!'

At the first word, the stampede began. Every man in that crowd streaked for shelter.

Careless shoved the reins into Ben's hands and shouted: 'Git goin', Ben! Drive through!'

Ben acted blindly on his leader's orders and lashed the horses into forward activity. They started to roll towards that spluttering brown-paper bundle.

Careless was standing up on top of the coach, feet among the parcels. A rope was swinging over his head. He threw it.

Fergie Allbright, just breathing a prayer of thanks as he got to an open doorway, felt a noose snatch around his chest, then he was dragged back into the street again.

He got his balance and turned, but the pull of the rope kept him running after the coach. He saw Careless grinning down at him, and realised that he was tied in a rope that was fastened to a rail on top of the coach.

Then the black-garbed man knew horror, for the first time in his life.

Those crazy fools were driving the careering coach straight on top of the spluttering dynamite bundle. But the horror really came when he

91

realised that he was going to be dragged over it, too!

He screamed in panic, and tried to free his arms, but he was helpless, being dragged along in the wake of the accelerating coach. He saw the coach make it in safety – saw the wheels pass over the bundle – and now it was his turn.

So Broken Knee heard the arrogant, powerful gambler, partner of the Big Mouth, screaming like a frightened child when he galloped on to that bundle, and then galloped past it, unharmed.

It just didn't blow up. And neither Burt Clay nor Ben could understand why big Careless O'Connor rolled around in his seat, roaring his head off with laughter.

A couple of hundred yards out of Broken Knee, with a baffled gang of gunnies unable to use snatched up rifles for fear of hitting their galloping, sweating, swearing leader in the rear of the old Concord, Careless recovered, wiped away tears of laughter and explained – 'That ain't dynamite! Jes' a fuse an' old paper!'

Careless had tricked the gunnies again.

SEVEN

THE UNSEEN ARMY!

When Yippee had stopped laughing, he wanted to know what to do with the enraged gambler, who was having to run faster than most men ever run in their lives.

Careless said: 'Haul him in. We ain't got time ter stop an' pick him up.'

So Ben hauled in the enraged gambler like a man pulling in a fish. He was just about a dead fish when finally they dragged him in to the footboard and then slung him into the coach. Careless clambered down, though it was dangerous at the speed they were travelling at and got inside with the gambler. He relieved him of his gun, taken from a shoulder holster, then sat back to wait for the man to recover.

It took him a long time. Fergie Allbright hadn't felt so bad in years.

Careless began the conversation. Gently. 'You know, you gotta pay fer ridin' in this coach. Nob'dy rides free, I figger.'

Allbright snarled, 'I didn't ask ter come.'

'Then why don't you get off?' – just as gently.

Fergie looked at the guns in Careless' holsters and decided he wouldn't try to get off the coach.

So Careless got down to questioning him.

'I told you I was comin' back ter Broken Knee ef only ter find out what happened ter Jim Whitfield, my pardner's brother.'

'Whitfield?'

'You know who I mean.' Careless was getting tougher in his tone now. 'I told you to have the information ready fer next time I came over. Wal, are you gonna talk?'

Fergie just sat in mean, brooding silence.

Careless reached out, grabbed a handful of black coat that wasn't so elegant now because of the powdery dust that was on it. He growled: 'You know what happened to the boy. Now open up that mouth an' talk."

Fergie snapped, 'An' ef I don't?'

'Ef you won't open your mouth, brother,' Careless growled as ferociously as he could, 'I'll open you up – plenty!' He shoved his big, battered face to within inches of Allbright's mean, glaring one.

'I'll fix you to a stick o' dynamite an' drop you on the trail.'

For one second Fergie's face registered horror.

Then he recovered. He was a gambler, and he thought he saw a bluff.

'Dynamite?' he sneered. 'Like that back in the town? I'll take a risk on that sort o' dynamite hurtin' me.'

Then Yippee roared down: 'Fer the love of Pete, Careless, them gunnies is sure catchin' up fast!'

Careless grabbed the gambler. Fergie started to struggle frantically, but he didn't have a chance inside that swaying, bumping coach, with big Careless operating on him. Within seconds he was hog-tied and helpless on the floor. He looked up, his eyes murderous, and saw the torn and shabby jeans pull up out of a window and drag on to the roof.

Ben, standing and urging the horses into their best pace, shouted: 'What're you goin' ter do, Careless? There's too many of 'em fer us to fight off.'

Careless slewed round, lying on top of the coach so as not to get thrown into the dust of the trail below. His eyes calculated, and then he said, comfortably: 'I figger we'll soon fix them varmints.'

He reached under his seat for another stick-like parcel. Ben said, sceptically: 'They won't fall fer that a second time, Careless.'

Careless drawled: 'Mebbe, Ben, but what else is there we c'n do?' And the logic was unanswerable.

A match spluttered, a fuse lit, died, then flared and gave off a stream of white smoke. Careless dropped the stick-like parcel on to the trail, and as it receded they saw it in plain view, fizzing away in the dust.

The approaching gunnies saw it, too, and the trio on top of the coach thought they even heard a yell of derision float after them. The gunnies were getting used to Careless' 'dynamite' by now.

But that dynamite suddenly exploded right in front of the string of galloping horsemen. All at once there was a vivid flash of flame, and then a swift, rolling roar of fury seemed to envelope the leading horsemen.

No one was actually hurt by the explosion, but it scared the life out of the highly-strung beasts. They turned into the thorn scrub and bolted, bucking and rearing and trying desperately to rid themselves of the weight in the saddles that restricted their dash away from that appalling noise.

It demoralised the pursuit, at least momentarily, and the old Concord went bucking and lurching down into the hollow, and then began the long, slow climb out of it.

By that time big Careless had shoved his faded blue jeans through the coach window again and hauled himself in beside his prisoner. He jerked the bound, desperate Fergie Allbright into an erect position in a corner, then sat down and faced him. He was handling another long, paper-wrapped stick, and Fergie, eyes starting from his head, saw the end of a fuse attached to it.

Careless said, easily: 'You figger my dynamite

ain't got no bump in it, huh?'

Fergie licked his lips. 'What're you gonna do, you big—'

Careless waited until the vituperation had stopped. For all his cussing, beads of sweat on Fergie's thin, mean face told of the fear that was in the man.

'I'm gonna blow the truth outa you, Allbright,' Careless told him. He leaned forward and tucked the stick down inside the bonds. Allbright nearly went mad, wrestling to get himself free, and finding that all his efforts were unavailing.

'You swine,' he gasped. 'You wouldn't dare do it!'

Fergie saw there was no bluff on that grim, brown face, and he licked his lips, and then said: 'Okay, I'll talk. That kid's out at the Crooked S.'

'The Crooked S?'

'David Simms' ranch.'

'It's a good name for it, then.' Careless didn't put away those matches. A face appeared at the window, upside down. Ginger hair steamed out as they raced along, and Careless reckoned the upside down head would be Ben's.

Ben shouted: 'That posse's after us agen. They're catchin' up fast, an' mighty mad, I reckon, now.'

Careless glanced out beyond Ben's head. He recognised the place. This was a narrow defile which led out of the hollow.

He told Ben, 'Quit worryin'. They'll never get

out of the pass, not this afternoon, I figger.' Ben pulled himself back and took the reins again from the injured Burt.

Still Careless didn't hurry. Instead he asked another question of Fergie. 'What are you doin' to him?'

'Jes' holdin' him prisoner.'

'Why?'

Sullenly: 'He wouldn't climb up an' drive outa town when we warned him that Broken Knee didn't want strangers. There's a limit ter what these Broken Knee folk'll stand, I guess. David Simms makes him do the chores around the ranch. He kicks him around plenty. Simms is that kind of fellar. Likes doin' it.'

There was another shout from above, and both caught the lashing of a whip as Ben tried to get more speed out of the straining horses, here in this ascending defile. Evidently the gunnies were closing rapidly behind them.

Careless knew he had no more time to waste.

'Allbright, I figger I'm gettin' on to your game, you an' the Big Mouth. It's all tied up with a raid by some Mexes on Neuces Bend a coupla days ago.' Allbright's eyes shot wide open at that. 'Wal, Mister Gambler, it's a dirty game – the dirtiest in the world – an' I'm aimin' ter stop it. For the moment, though, I figger you c'n lie an' think of all the harm an' sufferin' you an' your big-mouthed partner have caused along the Border.'

Before Allbright knew what he was doing

Careless had struck a match and applied it to the fuse. Allbright screamed as the saltpetre caught and spluttered into a flame that gave off a biting odour. He was shrieking for mercy, but Careless turned a hard face on him and wouldn't listen. It was time that Fergie Allbright, crooked gambler and worse, had to suffer. He kicked the door open against the wind, then pitched Allbright out on to the track. Almost in the same movement he pulled himself back on top of the coach again, slamming the door to with his foot.

Looking back he saw Allbright writhing frantically within his bonds to one side of the rutty trail. Right in front of the gambler's face was a spitting, burning fuse that burned closer to the stick-like parcel. The man must have been dying a thousand deaths with that burning train under his nose.

Farther beyond Allbright, the dust-covered posse had halted their horses, and were milling around uncertainly on the trail. The trouble was, in this defile there was no way of riding around the man on the trail – not if a man valued his life and wanted to keep at least fifty yards away from that deadly, menacing plume of smoke. Of course there wasn't a gunnie in that mob who was willing to risk his life to save his boss.

The coach pulled out of the depression and headed for the water hole across the mesa. The tired horses pulled at an easy canter now, and Ben and the wounded young Texan strained their ears to hear the last of Fergie Allbright.

Careless asked: 'What're you listenin' for?' – knowing darned well, of course.

'Waitin' fer the last a' Fergie,' Ben grated, and his eyes once again avoided Careless.

'Fergie?' Careless sounded shocked. 'Now, you wouldn't think I'd tie good dynamite to a worthless rogue like him, would you?'

Ben's head swung round, eyes goggling. 'Darn it, Careless, you don't mean—'

Confidentially Careless, sprawling back in his seat again, told them, 'Like the first parcel – jes' fuse an' paper. Won't harm him much I guess, but now he'll know what it feels like ter be threatened with death, like he an' his men have done so often.'

An incredulous town turned out to greet them, and when they saw three lazy, sprawling, cigarette-smoking *hombres* on top, hardly able to bother to hold the reins between them, they couldn't get over it. Cathy and Gracie were out to greet them, just as astonished, but infinitely more relieved.

Then they all dismounted. Ben said, awkwardly, 'Mebbe you'll come in, Careless.'

'Sure.' The big fellow didn't hesitate. Gracie caught his arm, smiling up into his face, and they all went in and had a meal. The past was over. Ben had found faith in the big, trampish looking *hombre* without the need for explanations.

Careless wasn't one to strain friendship, even so, and when darkness came he took the mesa trail on

100

his horse without telling anyone he was heading out of town.

When he rode into the vegetation that screened the water hole, he found the others were there before him. His horse shied and began to prance, and Careless got the smell of other horseflesh in among the bushes. Then he realised that everywhere around him were men.

Then Carlos spoke reassuringly from the darkness. 'Okay, O'Connor, you don't need to be afraid, senor.'

At that Careless relaxed and got down and someone took his horse away to the pickets. Everyone sat down. Carlos spoke. His voice was bitter.

'Things have become bad in our town, senor. The Big Mouth and his dozens of desperate gunmen have got the town completely in his power. This morning, just before your so-gallant stage arrived, the Big Mouth rode into town with all his men and forced our sons and young men to ride off with him.'

Careless sat up in the darkness. He was startled. 'Why?'

A growling voice took up the tale. 'We don't know why. It might be ter get our hot-blooded lads out of the way in case they start trouble. Or they might be kinda hostages for our good behaviour.'

'We're that much weaker,' the growling voice continued. 'All that's left is a passel of old men—'

'Old men, but we c'n fight,' shouted someone toughly.

'Fight? With our sons in the Big Mouth's power?' the old, growling voice demanded. 'We daren't stir fer fear o' what might be done to 'em – we daren't even ride into Laredo or Austin an' ask fer the Rangers ter come an' help. That Big Mouth's as crazy as a coot an' c'n do the most awful things ef he's got his mind set on it. I figger he's never bin right in his head since the Mexes came an' burned him out at the beginnin' o' the war.'

Careless interrupted quickly: 'Go on, old-timer, tell me more about that.' For he felt that he was getting a clue now to many mysteries.

But the old man was impatient and wouldn't give more than a few sentences in explanation of that part of David Simms' life.

'He was burned off his land. He lost everythin' in the fightin' an' got driven north ter Houston. They say he got shot up, too. We were told he enlisted with a Border force an' fought agen the Mexes, then, when it was all over, he came back an' started ter rebuild his place. But he sure hates them Mexes – that's why they call him the Big Mouth.'

'Because he's always shooting off what he'd like to do with 'em?'

'Sure. Always he starts ter rave about 'em, an' he certainly don't like 'em any.' Then the old man turned to more immediate problems. 'We kinda got a lot o' confidence in you, O'Connor.' A growl of approval swept the throng.

Carlos came back into the conversation. 'We figger, senor, if anyone can help us, it's you.'

Then everyone sat in silence, hopefully, as if expecting a miracle to happen and Careless O'Connor would hatch out a solution right there while they waited.

Careless sighed in protest. 'What c'n I do?'

That old growling voice said quickly, 'Find our sons fer us. Find what the Big Mouth an' his gunnies are doin' with 'em – an' get 'em away from him.'

'Jes' like that?' Careless' voice was ironical.

The old man said wearily: 'It's a lot ter ask, O'Connor, but c'n you see any way outa this mess fer us?'

O'Connor was listening. He thought someone was riding along the trail, hard. 'Mebbe. I figger in the end you c'n lick these crooks. The thing ter do is ter watch, night an' day, an' you c'n do that because you live in an' around Broken Knee. After a time we'll begin ter see their weaknesses, an' then we c'n strike back at 'em.'

The others had caught the sound of those fast-travelling hoofs, and were listening uneasily. Big Careless O'Connor went on talking, and they noticed that he gave orders like a man accustomed to telling people what to do.

'Fix your leaders, then put men on ter watch the Big Mouth an' Fergie. They're up ter somethin' –

when we know what it is, we c'n hit back at 'em. Every day the watchers must report to their leaders, an' every time I come into Broken Knee with the coach, that report should be passed on ter me.'

The lone horseman was coming down the last slope towards the trees around the water hole.

O'Connor said, 'Give me the names of your leaders – an' where is Simms' ranch?'

A sharp challenge halted the horseman, and they heard low voices talking. Around him, O'Connor heard the men elect the old man – a smallholder named Joseph Pugh – and Carlos Cordoves as their leaders.

Then they heard hoofs drumming through the trees towards them. Next instant the lone rider was right in their midst, pulling back on his horse's head and sending it rearing to an abrupt halt.

Pugh called, 'Who's that?'

'It's me – Red Duke.'

Carlos interrupted quickly, 'One o' my men.'

Duke called down to them. 'The Big Mouth's on the trail with all his men. They came ridin' through Broken Knee an hour after you left. I came over the bluffs' trail ter get here to warn you.'

Pugh called, 'Get your hosses, men, an' scatter. We'll meet termorrow at Carlos' place.'

There was a confusion of forms as men ran to identify their horses, then mount and gallop away into the desert off the trail.

O'Connor got his horse and climbed into the

saddle as it jumped into its stride. He swung up easily, them settled down to ride back to Neuces Bend.

About twenty minutes later, however, when he was still some miles from home, he began to hear a faint rumbling sound in the desert behind him. It grew louder, and suddenly he sat up, stiffening. That noise was being made by horsemen! It sounded like an army riding the trail towards Neuces Bend.

EIGHT

THE CROOKED S RANCH

He came to the fork in the trail, where the straight track went on to the Rio Grande and the Border, and the Neuces Bend trail circled off to the right.

O'Connor took the Neuces Bend trail, but rode it only for a hundred yards or so. Then he pulled into the scrub off the track and sat his horse to await the arrival of the approaching party.

The drumming noise grew louder, then the leaders of the horsemen swept into view, a series of black shadows silhouetted against the silvery night sky. They didn't turn; they were riding away from him, down the trail that led to the Border. At least a hundred riders were in that party – maybe even nearer two hundred. And this was a gringo party.

There was nothing now between them and the

Border – there was no object except Mexico ahead for the men from Broken Knee. And what was there in Mexico for armed men, riding by night?

Careless knew, and his face in the moonlight was as hard as it had ever looked.

He hooked one torn trousered leg across his saddle, rolled himself a curly and did some heavy thinking. When his cigarette was only halfway through, he had made up his mind.

He turned his horse away from Neuces Bend and rode through the night towards Broken Knee. He circled the town, however, and eventually found himself alongside the dreary waste that was the Big Mouth's ranch.

His horse clop-clopped softly up the dirt track. Ahead of him he saw an ugly huddle of ranch buildings, and a snaking line of corral posts. He came towards the shadow of the first building, a long barn alongside the dirt track. A voice suddenly rang out, a quick growl, like that of a man who has been caught napping,

Careless remembered the hundred-odd men who had ridden away from the Crooked S that night and didn't bother to disguise his voice. He was sure he wouldn't be recognised.

He said, disgusted: 'That blame critter went lame on me, ten miles back. Me, I've bin walkin' most of the night.' He got down. He could see a shadowy figure against the darker gloom of the barn wall. There was a rifle in the man's hand, and it was pointing at Careless.

O'Connor behaved naturally under the circumstances. He stretched his limbs with a sigh of relief, and, anyway, they were stiff enough after so many hours in the saddle.

Careless put a world of weariness into his voice. 'Me, I ran outa matches, an' I ain't had no smoke all night an' I'm dyin' fer a curly.'

Deftly rolling a cigarette, he ambled stiffly across towards the rifleman. Obligingly the man put down his gun and fumbled for a match.

O'Connor let him strike it, let him bring the glowing light right in towards his face. His big, flat pan was grinning as he looked over the cupped hands at the watcher.

He saw an unshaven jowl, a lumpish face with weary eyes looking at him. Then the weariness went with a yelp of surprise. The watcher had recognised O'Connor.

That yelp was the last squeak out of him. O'Connor's hands fastened about that massive, fleshy neck, and then suddenly the man went swinging in an arc and crashed head first against the wall of the barn.

He was out when O'Connor knelt beside him. When he recovered consciousness a few minutes later, O'Connor had gone, but he felt no desire to go off after him.

For O'Connor had taken a lace out of the man's boot and had fastened his thumbs behind his back, with one foot hooked between his hands. So long as he lay still it didn't hurt much, but the slightest effort to change his position or get his thumbs free brought with it an agony that was excruciating.

O'Connor had learned that trick from the Apache Indian wars.

He rode quite boldly up to the ranch-house. There was an oil lamp burning inside a building he guessed to be the bunkhouse, as if other men sat awake in case of need.

He dismounted and let the reins drag in case of need for a quick getaway. Then he went and had a look in at the cookhouse window.

No one opened up at him as his head came in front of the dirty windowpane. Inside he saw the usual cookhouse, with its big wood-burning stove across one end on which was an array of pans, and not-to-clean tables down the centre of the room.

Three men were inside. One was hacking off slices of bacon and slapping them into a sizzling frying-pan. Another was stirring a pot full of beans. The third man sat across by the door with a rifle on his lap.

Careless looked at the two cooks. After a while he decided that the man slapping bacon into the frying-pan was Grace's brother, Jim. That made his heart jump, for he'd come all this way in the hope of getting him free from the Big Mouth's clutches.

He studied him. He was taller than Grace, of course, but the likeness to the girl was consider-able, and Careless felt that he was not mistaken. Blue eyes and a tumbling thatch of blond hair – he was a Whitfield, all right.

Suddenly his attention was drawn to the boy at the big pan by the stove. His head had come round, and he was glaring at the guard in a very malevolent manner. The guard looked up and at once the boy went back to his stirring.

Careless thought, 'Hully gee, that kid sure has had a beatin' up!' And he wondered why.

Then he heard sounds across in the bunkhouse. Someone was stamping around and calling. Maybe a foreman rousing the men for the day's chores around the ranch.

Careless walked to the cookhouse door, and as he approached he signalled his arrival by whistling a night-herder's song – 'Huile, huile, palomita.'

He came into the cookhouse openly advertising his approach; for he guessed that he'd get a rifle bullet at him if he tried to sneak up quietly into the place. As it was, so sure was he that the whistler was a friend, the guard with the rifle didn't bother to take his face out of the coffee pot as the cookhouse door opened.

When he did come up gasping for air, he looked into a blue-eyed Colt – and the rifle was still across his lap.

Careless took the coffee pot out of the man's nerveless hand. 'You don't need that as much as I do,' he said gently, and while his Colt pointed unwaveringly at the startled man on the chair, he got his stomach around the thick, sweet liquid. It did him good.

The young fellow at the bean pot must have

heard a sound, for his head came stiffly, painfully round again. His eyes tried to open wide behind the puffy flesh, astonished at sight of the big tramp of a *hombre* holding up the armed guard at the door.

Then he dropped his wooden spoon and came lurching across, wiping his hands dry on his jeans. O'Connor saw that bruised face look up in his, registering astonishment – and delight.

'The heck, it's you – the stagecoach man,' the kid exclaimed.

The guard came to his senses at that moment. He set his chair on all four legs again with a crash, and came lumbering to his feet. O'Connor dropped the pot and whisked the rifle away from him.

The guard's voice was incredulous. 'You've got a nerve, O'Connor, comin' here. Davey Simms'll grind you ter dust when he knows you've bin a-gunnin' here.'

The kid with the battered face reached for the rifle. 'Gimme that gun,' he said, 'I wanta kill some-b'dy.'

Careless kept hold of the rifle. 'Mebbe I don't want anybody killin' yet,' he said mildly. He looked at the blond-headed young man. 'You Jim Whitfield?' The man nodded and began to come across. 'I've come fer you, then. Go get a hoss an' we'll ride off to your sister.'

'What?' Jim Whitfield's expression was incredulous. 'The heck, you mean I c'n leave this place at last?'

His expression was sufficient. Evidently Jim Whitfield had loathed having to be chore boy to the Crooked S outfit.

The kid with the battered face made another grab for the rifle. Careless shoved him away.

'Mister, I've taken all I'm gonna take from any man,' the kid said. 'They wanted me ter ride off with the filibusters, but I was one of the boys who said we wouldn't ride. The Big Mouth sicked three fellars on to me. They beat me till I couldn't stand, after which the other boys kinda changed their minds an' rode off with the filibusters.'

'By which time you couldn't ride a hoss, so they had ter leave you behind?' queried Careless softly, watching that battered young face before him.

'Yeah. But the swine threw me out of my bunk an hour ago ter help make breakfast for 'em.' The little eyes were watching that rifle, fascinated. It meant a lot to the kid, that gun. With it he could wipe out the pain and indignity of that savage mauling.

Jim Whitfield shoved out past the man at the door. Careless looked at the kid with the battered face. 'Ain't you gonna go an' git yourself a hoss?'

'Okay,' growled the boy. His eyes kept looking at that rifle, then at one of the guard's Colts. The guard at the door didn't miss the expression, either.

His hands were high in the air. He called to Careless, 'Mister, you keep the kid away from my guns. There's no sayin' what he'll do ef he gets his hand around a butt.' He was alarmed.

'You don't need many guesses ter figger what he'd do with a gun,' Careless returned dryly. All the same he said, 'Keep away from that fellar's Colt, son, or I'll sure put a bullet through your hand.' He wasn't going to have any premature fireworks which would arouse the rest of the men on the ranch.

The kid stalked out at that. It was almost daylight outside. Careless wanted the boys to hurry, because he knew any time now the punchers would be coming in for chow.

While he was waiting, the door swung open and a man walked in. His right arm was in a sling. He wore a belt that was highly ornamented with Mexican silver, and he was a dude right down to his hand-tooled riding boots.

But Careless knew him immediately. It was the *hombre* who had called him a dingo-lover, back in the saloon in Neuces Bend – and had been shot through his arm in attempting to follow the insult with lead.

'Rope!' exclaimed the man who had been guarding the cookhouse prisoners, and Careless remembered that his former opponent had been called Rope Curry.

Curry's eyes went wide, then narrowed.

Careless said, gently, 'Come an' join us, fellar. Don't make any sound while you do, though.' His Colt waggled.

Rope Curry and the other scrub-faced man

stood, faces lowering, hands above their heads, and waited.

Then they heard hoofs, muffled by the thick dusty soil outside, come clumping to the cookhouse. Whitfield came in. He looked at Careless. 'They're movin' about now,' he said hurriedly. 'Let's get outa here quick.' He had courage, but he didn't want any more days of captivity here on the Crooked S.

The door opened again behind him, and the kid with the battered face came in. He suddenly leapt behind the wounded gunnie and whipped out his Colt. They saw the triumph in his puffed-up, blackened eyes as he felt the weight of the gun.

'Stop that,' exclaimed Careless quickly. His gun swept round. 'Put that gun away an' let's get outa here.'

'You try'n stop me,' the kid gritted. He was dragging the wounded Rope Curry back with him towards the door, using the helpless gunnie as a shield. Careless couldn't shoot, even if he had wanted to. Before he could make up his mind what to do, the young Texan had kicked open the door, hurled Curry back into the room and fled.

Careless jumped towards the door. 'C'mon,' he shouted to Whitfield. 'All Hades is gonna pop in a minute.'

It did. They leapt into their saddles, just as the shooting started. They heard guns blasting off down in the bunkhouse. The kid must have walked boldly in and started shooting.

Careless threw the captured rifle across to Jim Whitfield. 'Beat it,' he called, though he wheeled his own horse in the direction of the bunkhouse. Whitfield didn't say anything, but just turned his horse and followed him. For all his fear of being taken prisoner again, Whitfield wasn't going to run out and leave the kid to fight this battle alone.

Careless approved. He rated Grace's brother high after that. They crashed at headlong speed down to where the war was raging.

There must have been a dozen gunnies hidden up among the buildings, and they ripped off as the horsemen flashed by. Fortunately they were racing at such speed that they were behind the barns before their opponents could take proper aim.

They saw the kid suddenly bolt from the wide-open doors of a shed. They wheeled their horses towards him. Then the men back of them began to rip off with their rifles. They got the kid and he staggered, then somehow he found strength and came running on again.

They pulled up, almost on top of him. Careless looked down into that pain-wracked face and realised that the kid couldn't climb into his saddle.

Big Careless O'Connor flung himself off his horse, grabbed the kid and threw him into his saddle. Then he slapped the skittish beast and sent it away like a racehorse from the starting line.

His own horse had started to gallop away without him, but O'Connor put his long legs into a run and came leaping into the saddle from behind. He wasn't going to be left on the Crooked S by any nervous horse, he thought grimly. It wouldn't be nice to be caught by this mob of vengeful gunnies. Rope Curry and that fellow with his thumbs Apache-tied would sure be mean to him.

The three riders hurtled round the back of the buildings. They had to come in a circle to regain the dirt track and the way out from the ranch, and that put them under fire from the buildings alongside the bunkhouse.

They got away riding like mad to get beyond rifle range, and then settled down to a more lasting pace on the road into Broken Knee. After a while they realised that three or four gunnies were closing in on them, their horses fresh from the night's rest. O'Connor turned at that and waited for them to come up and the two boys halted behind him.

O'Connor said, 'You go on. Your hosses is fresh.'

Whitfield said, 'You saved us, brother. We don't leave you now.'

So they waited. Four gunnies suddenly saw three resolute men in their path. They saw that one of them was O'Connor!

Their horses lost speed. Then they halted. The riders conferred, and then turned their mounts and rode back the way they had come. They weren't going to take on big Careless O'Connor, not when a dozen Allbright gunnies had failed to best him!

The boys grinned and started to turn to resume their way, but O'Connor wasn't moving yet. He was looking back to where the huddle of buildings proclaimed the Crooked S ranch.

He called, 'Kid, what did you do in that blamed barn, jes' afore you ran out to meet us?'

The kid shuffled uncomfortably in his saddle. His voice came hoarsely, 'What d'you mean? I didn't do anythin'.'

Careless said, softly, 'You set fire to that barn, didn't you, kid?'

His finger was pointing. A dense cloud of smoke was hanging over the ranch buildings. They sat and watched, and saw the flames go higher as building after building took fire.

Careless sighed after a time. 'I thought I'd seen the last of farms bein' burned along the Border,' he said. 'Looks like the Crooked S is goin' to be blackened fer the second time in three or four years.'

Whitfield let out his breath as if he had been holding it, aghast. 'When the Big Mouth sees his ranch like that a second time, he'll sure take Broken Knee ter pieces an' everybody in it, out of revenge. You don't know that Big Mouth fellar. Lay a finger on him, an' he goes crazy. He'll make a lot of people suffer for this.'

NINE

CARELESS RIDES!

The kid sat hunched on his horse. It looked far too big for him. He talked tough, though, for a seventeen-year-old.

'You fellars gripin' at me fer doin' it? The heck, no passel o' danged coyotes beats the daylights outa me an' gets away with it!'

Careless soothed, 'Sure kid, we know how you feel. I guess we'd all go plumb crazy fer revenge ef we'd been knocked around like you've been treated. I guess it had ter come, sometime.'

He started along the trail towards Broken Knee, but at the foot of the long climb that led over the hill to the town he paused again. He said, 'We'll part here, fellars. Jim an' me will hightail it across the mesa fer Neuces Bend. You go on into Broken Knee, kid; find old Joseph Pugh an' tell him what happened. Tell him I'll be ridin' in with the coach every day from now on.'

'Every day?' The kid puckered bruised lips as if to whistle, found that it hurt and changed his mind. 'You know what I figure?'

The big, tattered fellow shook his head, wondering what was coming.

'I figure you're up to some game – somep'n deep! An' the Big Mouth an' all these other no-good *hombres* c'n look to themselves!'

With that he spurred away. Jim Whitfield looked curiously at his companion as they turned out across the rolling mesa. He queried, 'Anythin' in that?'

Careless grinned mockingly. 'I never play any games,' he retorted, then changed the subject.

As they went into Neuces Bend, the younger man told him what had happened to himself. It was much as Fergie Allbright had said – the Big Mouth had thought it something to have a chore boy, someone for everyone to kick around.

'And they sure kicked me around,' Jim Whitfield said. 'That bunch is sure the orneriest collection o' spiteful vipers I ever set eyes on. Then that kid opened his mouth too much, and they pitched into him instead.'

He told the kid's story, as it had been told to him. The previous morning the Big Mouth had sent his men into Broken Knee with instructions to bring in as many of the tough young men as they could round up.

'Why?' asked Careless softly.

120

Jim Whitfield was rolling a cigarette. He paused and looked at big Careless. 'You don't know?' He licked the gum edge of his paper, then lit up. 'You're the cause of it. When Fergie Allbright twice came out an' said you'd bested him an' his men, it made the Big Mouth take fright. He figgered that your success would give the citizens of Broken Knee the heart to fight back agen him, an' he reckoned the danger would come from the younger men.'

'So he dragged 'em all in? Why did he take 'em with him, tonight?'

The young man drew deeply, gratefully, on his cigarette. Careless realised then that part of the Big Mouth's meanness had been to deprive a smoker of his cigarettes.

'I reckon he figgered they might get up to tricks ef they were left back at the ranch with only a few guards. But also, I figger he's tryin' ter make 'em in hock like the rest of his men.'

'You mean, ef they're made ter go filibusterin', that makes 'em filibusters just like him an' his men, an' afterwards they've got ter sink or swim with him?'

Jim blew out smoke, gratefully. They jogged along, the morning sun in their eyes. He said, tiredly, 'So you know the Big Mouth's dirty game?'

'Filibsterin'?' Careless nodded. He'd nearly had enough, and was swaying with weariness in his saddle. 'Yeah, I've guessed it for a while.'

Jim said, dryly, 'You don't get news easily outa

Broken Knee. That's how they kept things quiet so long, I reckon. An' that's why they didn't exactly welcome a stage line.'

It all added up, now that Careless knew for certain that back of everything was filibustering.

It had been one of the greatest evils of the war with Mexico, the development of the filibuster. Small companies of Texans had waged private wars across the Border, raiding and fighting pitched battles with the Mexicans, laying siege to villages and even towns of considerable size and sacking them and riding away in triumph with whatever loot they could capture.

Inevitably Mexican marauders had struck back, burning and pillaging on Texan land, and this had given excuse for further filibustering expeditions.

Jim didn't speak again until they were almost into Neuces Bend. Then he said, abruptly, 'Who are you, Careless?'

Careless retorted, mildly, 'Find out, son.' And then they were walking slowly down into a town that had just risen from its bed.

Few people saw them as they dismounted outside Wrigleys. Ben was in the store, and he came forward in astonishment at sight of the travel-stained pair.

'Fer land's sake,' he exclaimed, his red hair almost standing on end, 'you look to have bin in the saddle all night, Careless.'

He looked curiously at the blond stranger who followed behind the big fellow. Careless said, 'This is Gracie's brother, Jim.' And then Grace herself came, stared incredulously, and then ran for joy into her brother's arms.

'After this,' she said, some minutes later, 'I'll believe anything's possible of you, you big cow-wrangler!' She was near to tears, but they were tears of delight.

She hugged the torn-shirted cowboy in an ecstasy of gratitude. Lean, rangy Burt was lounging in the doorway, chewing on a straw. When he saw Careless getting all the attention, he threw down the stalk disgustedly and asked, 'Why can't I rescue her brother occasionally?'

His worship of the big, resourceful, casual-looking fellar removed any jealousy from his mind. But he couldn't help feeling mournful when he saw Careless get the attentions he so much desired for himself.

Within half an hour of his getting down to sleep, Careless had to be wakened.

A solitary rider came spurring in from Broken Knee – a messenger from the citizens' committee over there. They showed him round to where Careless lay in the corner.

Careless sat up, his eyes suspicious. He didn't recognise the *hombre*. But the messenger's words were convincing.

'Joe Pugh sent me. You know old Joe? Him we fixed up with Carlos to lead the citizens agen the Big Mouth.' He drank noisily, wiped his dripping mouth with the back of his hand, then said, 'Joe figgers trouble's gonna come mighty quick now, Careless. That's why he told me ter ride openly into Neuces Bend – now it don't matter who knows we're linked up with you!'

Careless climbed up off the sacks. 'What d'you mean by that, brother?'

'I mean, a fellar went ridin' off as soon as it was light from the burnt-out Crooked S ranch. He was ridin' hell-fer-leather, an' takin' the Border trail.'

'I see.' Careless got it at once. Someone had gone after big David Simms – the Big Mouth – to tell him of the disaster that had occurred to his ranch in his absence.

Careless said, softly, 'I wonder how the Big Mouth's gonna feel when he knows his ranch is gutted for the second time. He's gonna be mighty sore.'

The messenger stood up. 'He's gonna be mighty mad.' He drank again. 'An' I ain't kiddin',' he went on, his voice growling.

'Mebbe so.' Careless was getting down on the sacks again. 'Tell Pugh I'm restin' up today. But tell him I'll make a trip over tomorrow. Tell him to watch out – when the Big Mouth returns he'll sure go on the rampage an' take Broken Knee apart. If I was Pugh I'd go an' clean up any of the Big Mouth's gang that are left in Broken Knee. Like that gamblin' man, Fergie Allbright, an' his friends.'

The messenger shook his head doubtfully, uncertainly. 'That's easy ter say,' he growled. 'But the Big Mouth's got a lot of young men as hostages, don't fergit.'

Careless just said, comfortably, 'You do as I say, brother. It's time we started smackin' back at the Big Mouth an' not worryin' too much about what he c'n do agen us.'

That evening a deputation rode over from Broken Knee. Joseph Pugh led it. Careless was found at the coach, patching up and preparing for the next day's run into Broken Knee.

Joe called, 'Howdy, Careless.'

The big fellar read the signs of desperation on those weather-bronzed features. 'Somep'n kinda bitin' you,' he said.

They dismounted. 'Somep'n sure is,' growled old Joe Pugh. 'A dozen of us walked in on Fergie Allbright's gamblin' parlour. We rounded the lot up. Then we rode out ter Simms' ranch, the Crooked S, an' collected another seven or eight mavericks. But I reckon we ain't happy.'

'About your boys?' Careless asked softly. He could understand their feelings.

'Sure. There's fourteen of our young men in the power o' them doggoned gunnies,' gritted Pugh. 'What's the Big Mouth gonna do to 'em when he knows we've started to fight back agen him?' he suddenly exploded. Plainly old Joe was feeling bad, but then one of his sons was in the power of the filibusters.

The other men started to talk now, all growling their discontent and anxiety.

125

'Look,' said Careless, and his voice had the ring of steel in it. 'I know how you feel. But there's no other way, don't you see? That Big Mouth plays a deep game, an' one of the boys I rescued says it was Simms' idea to make your sons filibusters like his own men. Then you'd never be able to do anythin' agen him because if so you'd be doin' it agen your own boys – they'd be part of his gang. So I figger, then, settin' fire to the Simms' ranch was a good thing after all. It sent a rider off after the Big Mouth, an' he'll call off his raid an' that means he won't make killers an' robbers of your sons.'

Joe brightened. 'That's somep'n,' he admitted. Then his face fell. 'But that don't get our boys outa the power o' that crazy, killin' Mex-hater, David Simms. An' right now I figger the filibusters are headin' back fer Broken Knee as fast as hoofs c'n bring 'em.'

Careless said, 'You don't need to worry, fellars. Just leave things ter me. Let the Big Mouth bring your boys safely back over the Border, an' then mebbe we c'n find a way of persuadin' him ter part with 'em.'

Partly reassured, the men began to climb back into their saddles. They had an immense faith in the big, fighting cowboy.

Careless wandered in on the Wrigleys when it was time for supper. During the meal he told Yippee, 'Tomorrow, old hoss, you take the coach into Broken Knee. Mebbe Jim an' Ben will travel with you, but you won't need 'em.'

'You figger it'll be safe?' Burt reluctantly tore his eyes away from dainty, graceful Gracie Whitfield. 'What about that gamblin' man an' his toughies?'

Careless told them the news. 'The citizens' committee have jumped 'em an' taken 'em all prisoners. They're in revolt at last agen the Big Mouth. It had to come some time, I reckon. Only—'

They all looked at him. Cathy stopped ladling out the food and said, softly, 'What's on your mind, big man?'

He said, 'The Big Mouth's got a lot of hostages, the young men from Broken Knee. He c'n smash any resistance from the citizens with them in his power.'

Everyone looked uncomfortable at the news, and their jubilation swiftly disappeared. Unhappily Grace asked, 'What advice did you give, Careless?'

'I told 'em to fight.' When they looked at the big man his face was a mask of fighting grimness. 'The heck, they've got to fight, sooner or later, so why not now?'

'Right now, with those boys in his power?' Ben stared. This didn't add up.

'Listen,' Careless told them. 'Stop kidding yourself. The Big Mouth could smash any resistance from the Broken Knee citizens without havin' ter use any hostages. He's got over a hundred trained killers behind him, an' they're a match for several times that number of farmers an' traders an' men who don't live by their guns. Them hostages just makes things kinda more complicated.'

127

Cathy spoke to him later, when he was saddling his horse. 'I don't understand, Careless. But' – she smiled a grand smile at him as he mounted – 'I reckon you're right, whatever you do. Now tell me where you're going?'

He grinned. 'I'm goin' ter see that the Big Mouth doesn't win,' he told her.

TEN

CHECKMATE!

Ben drove the coach into Broken Knee rather early the following morning. On top, with him, rode Burt and Jim, both nursing rifles and keeping a sharp watch out in spite of Careless reassurances. But the journey into Broken Knee was uneventful – Careless, they said, was always right.

They didn't carry passengers on the outward journey, but there were some women and children to be brought back from Broken Knee. The citizens expected big trouble, and they wanted the weak and helpless out of the way when it came.

Broken Knee was an armed camp. The citizens' committee had sent to the outlying ranches for all available assistance, and there had been many riders into the town that morning, though most were uneasy and grumbled about the situation.

Burt heard some of the growling as he strode

along the board sidewalk.

'What'n heck have we got ter shove our noses in for?' someone snapped. 'Davy Simms never did anythin' agen us, not unless we went interferin' into his business.'

Burt snapped back, 'He packed that cemetery with pretty good citizens, didn't he? Him an' his imported gunnies.'

'Wal, I still figger we're gonna regret takin' a stand agen Simms,' the spokesman growled. 'I figger that O'Connor fellar gave bad advice. We didn't ought to have pulled in Fergie an' then gone out ter Simms' ranch an' took them other rannies prisoner!'

He checked himself, as a thought came to him, and his eye brightened excitedly. But someone else had butted in on the conversation. It was another *hombre* who was so worried that he didn't consider his words.

'Looks like O'Connor don't give a darn what happens to Broken Knee so long as his precious Mexes don't get hurt,' he shouted, and at that the old cry went up – something they'd learned from Rope Curry and the other prisoners, maybe. 'Mebbe he's not called a renegade fer nothin'. Mebbe he's playin' a deep game, that Careless *hombre*!'

Burt snarled, 'You make me tired! There isn't a fellar here that's fit ter lick his boots, an' he ain't no renegade, I tell yer. I've also got a dozen li'l pieces o' lead that'll back my arguments any time anyone says renegade again!'

He was crouching, hands hovering over his Colts, a young man incensed because of the words spoken against his idol. Ben grabbed him and pulled him away, just as the group began to look more hostile. 'Get on to that coach, fellar. We want ter help Broken Knee folk, not fight 'em.'

Jim caught hold of Burt's other arm and they led the young Texan away between them. As they passed out of earshot, that man with the excited gleam in his eye began to talk to two or three cronies. The trio, walking away to their loaded coach, didn't know it, but those men, to save their own hides, were planning treachery on the defenders at Broken Knee.

They were just pulling out of the plaza, when a rider came in from the south in a flurry of dust and small stones.

The rider, sweating, caked with dust from the trail, lifted himself in his saddle and shouted, 'The Big Mouth's crossed the Rio. They'll be here in two or three hours!'

It was one of the scouts posted on the Border by Joe Pugh to watch for the return of the filibusters.

Joe shouted, 'What about our boys? Did you see 'em in the party?'

The scout nodded, trying to get his breath. 'They're with the Big Mouth, all right. He's got 'em tied in their saddles, an' they've each got a noose round their necks, Injun fashion, to keep 'em from tryin' ter escape ef there's an attack.'

That shocked the people there, many of them

131

parents of the prisoners. That was how Comanches rode through hostile country with prisoners; in case of attack, the prisoners were the first to die, being jerked from their horses by those tightening nooses and dragged to their death by the savage Indian captors.

'What c'n we do now to save our boys?' someone shouted in panic. 'We can't lick that Big Mouth no how, an' we was fools even ter think of it.'

Then someone shouted, 'Where's that Careless O'Connor critter? There's bin nothin' but trouble ever since he started ter run that coach into Broken Knee. Simms was right, coaches only bring people – an' trouble!'

Then that rider lifted up his head and told them where Careless was.

'He's ridin' with the Big Mouth an' his party!'

Three men came shoving forward at that, snarling and ready to fight the town rather than listen to such talk against the man they worshipped.

'What d'you mean by that?' shouted Burt Clay, but the man just shook his head wearily and said, 'Fellar, I ain't tellin' you no untruth. What I'm sayin' I saw with my own eyes. When they came ridin' through the Rio, Careless was right in among the party.'

It shocked the trio, for they felt that this was an honest man delivering a plain testimony of what he had seen. But a bigger shock was to come to them.

132

The scout from the Border said, 'What's more, O'Connor was one of the fellars holdin' on to a rope around the neck of one of our boys – your'n, Joe Pugh, your Dan'l!'

By dawn that morning, Careless O'Connor was over the broad Rio Grande and a mile or two into Mexican territory. It was territory hostile to solitary gringos, but the big man didn't count on much danger, for few Mexicans lived so close to the troublesome Border these days, and the place was a waste with burnt out villages everywhere.

Shortly after nine in the morning, so far as he could judge by the sun, he saw the first signs of the returning filibusters. They were a weary lot, as if they had been riding through the night, and their pace was little more than a walk down the rough trail into the gorge where the ford was.

Careless came riding down a small valley so that he fell in with the party at the rear. He took a chance on being recognised, but he thought that if he kept well back, with his head down, like a tired man on a horse going lame, no one would get interested in him.

No one was interested. Probably no one so much as looked back once, anyway, and would have been too jaded to have identified their enemy riding so openly and boldly on the heels of the cavalcade.

On the edge of the ford a shouted word to halt floated back down the column of horsemen. Then it was that Careless realised that a small bunch of riders in the centre of the party was unarmed – were in fact, prisoners, surrounded by heavily-armed gunmen.

Careless heard a shouted instruction for the prisoners to be kept to the rear, now that they were entering Texas territory, and be led 'Comanche'.

He knew what being led 'Comanche' meant, and when he saw the young men being bound in their saddles, he took even greater risk and shoved his way in among them. Some of the tired fili-busters were sending their rope's nooses spinning round the necks of the helpless boys, and on an impulse Careless tossed his rope, too.

Then the cavalcade took to the water, leaving the men with the prisoners to bring up the rear – and Careless took care to enure that he was last man of all with the prisoners.

The boy – a tough young Texan of about nine-teen – had gasped at sight of Careless, when the big man pulled him back alongside him, but the grim grey eyes just lifted in a meaning look and the kid had sense to go silent immediately.

They splashed through the water and then took to the trail back through the foothills towards the Neuces basin. The pace was still very slow, because of the tired horses, and bound though they were, the prisoners kept up close behind the main body.

This worried Careless and he made no move until close on noon. Then another shouted order came floating down the column to them. It was something about 'break the trail', and it was an order to the men with the prisoners to perform this work and then catch up as hurriedly as possible with the main party, who would wait for them at a point overlooking Broken Knee.

Careless didn't understand it, but he was relieved to see the leading horsemen put on a little speed and draw gradually away from them. By the grumbling, Careless gathered that the men with the prisoners didn't relish the task allotted to them.

The main column had loped straight along the trail towards Broken Knee, but when the bunch including the prisoners came to the fork, they turned left towards Neuces Bend.

Careless was bewildered. He couldn't understand this manoeuvre. Half a mile along the track, however, the leaders of the little party suddenly pulled round on the rocky trail and went riding back over their traces again. It was a bad moment for Careless, this unexpected manoeuvre, for it brought him almost face to face with the Crooked S gunnies. Probably the only thing that saved him from recognition was the fact that all the manoeuvring threw up a blinding cloud of alkali dust so that no one saw anyone very plainly in those few crowded seconds. Careless breathed a sigh of relief, all the same, when the danger passed and the column was strung out as before.

Then he began to move. He decided the time was ripe; it was risky, but then to win he knew he would have to take risks.

He kept his eye on the gunnie with the prisoner just ahead, while he slipped a knife behind his own prisoner's back and slit his bonds for him. As the knife bit into the tough cord he felt the kid stiffen, at first not able to believe what was happening. Then he caught the delight in the boy's eye and winked at him and motioned to keep quiet.

When the kid's hands were free he stuck the knife-handle into his fingers and let him cut away the ropes that fastened his legs under his horse's belly.

By this time they had rejoined the main Border trail from Broken Knee, and Careless was beginning to understand the manoeuvre. Some of the men with spare ropes at once threw them over thorn bushes and pulled them out of the earth and let them tow out behind them.

Careless saw that this way the marks of a big posse of horsemen were obliterated, and anyone following behind would think that the column had, in fact, turned left and headed for Neuces Bend and not gone on to Broken Knee.

A fierce, welling anger surged within him when he understood the trick. It explained that ferocious onslaught by the Mexicans upon Neuces Bend recently. The Big Mouth's filibusters must have practised this manoeuvre before, must have laid a false trail towards Neuces Bend after one of their raids, and some tracking Mexican must have followed it and deduced that the filibusters came from that town and not from Broken Knee.

So that vengeful raid had been brought upon an innocent community by the misdoings of the Broken Knee filibusters!

Under cover of the dust cloud that the trailing thorn bushes threw up, Careless pushed his horse forward until he drew level with the guard ahead. As he rode he beckoned to the kid with the knife to close up on the prisoner.

A begrimed cowboy, dust coating his lashes and eyebrows, so that he had to peer out between nearly closed lids, saw a hulking shape ride up alongside him.

His hat nearly fell off as his head jerked up in astonishment. Sure he'd seen that face before, that big, flat, fighting face. His hands started to travel. But Careless beat him to the draw.

That prisoner was swiftly released, then Careless dragged out the Crooked S rannie's two Colts and handed them to the kids.

The next rannie up the line swallowed his plug when a thing that felt like a gun barrel rammed into his ribs from behind. It was a gun barrel. Careless left him and his prisoner to the attention of the newly released kids, and went up the line and stuck up the next *hombre*.

They played the game half a dozen times more, and then Careless got tired of it. He suddenly rode boldly right up among the five men who were left and said, 'Where do you guys think you're headin'?'

They were so startled, they didn't understand who this trail-dusty tramp of a fellow was for a second. Then they halted and looked round.

They saw nine of their companions, sullen and out of temper, sitting back along the trail under the guard of three of the former prisoners. And sitting in a line right behind their five backs were six tough-looking young Texans, each armed with Colts.

The leader sighed and lifted his hands, and at that the other Crooked S rannies followed suit. It was victory without a shot being fired.

Now it was the rannies' turn to be 'Coman-ched', and they were led away by four of the boys into Neuces Bend for safe keeping.

As they took the trail again into Broken Knee, Careless got the story from the boys. He learned that the one he had led Comanche-fashion was Danny Pugh, old Joe's son, and it was from him, mostly, that Careless learned what had happened.

'The Big Mouth was goin' ter make us take part in a raid,' Danny confirmed, 'so's never afterwards could anyone in Broken Knee take action agen him without hurtin' us. But just when we were startin' business, just at dusk a fellar comes ridin' in from the Crooked S sayin' the ranch had been gutted.'

Careless said, 'I figger the Big Mouth shot off some at that,' with a grin.

The kid lifted his hands. 'You ain't said the half of it! He nearly fell off his hoss, he was so good an' mad. We'd bin all set ter raid a Mexican village about thirty miles inland – a place with a mission which looked as if it might have plenty silver work inside it. The only trouble was, we'd bin seen an' we

138

could expect ter have ter make a big fight fer it."

'You were seen?' Careless became interested.

'Yeah.' The boy eased his horse over some rough ground and then said, 'Suddenly, just on dark, the bell began to toll in that mission tower – rapidly, an' we knew it was an alarm. One of our scouts came ridin' back ter say there was big parties of Mexes ridin' in from all the countryside.

'Ef we'd have ridden in to attack, right there and then, we'd have ransacked the place afore the reinforcements arrived, I guess, but just at that moment up rides this fellar from the Crooked S and takes the Big Mouth's mind clean off'n fili-busterin'. Nobody touches anythin' belongin' Davy Simms an' lives, I reckon,' he ended grimly.

But Careless had other questions to ask. 'What happened to the Mexes?'

'I don't know.' The boy shrugged. 'We rode hard through the night, an' it was dark, so they wouldn't be able to trail us. Maybe,' he added, 'they might have come after us with dawn, when they could track us.'

'And it was a big gathering of Mexicans,' Careless said, but it was more to himself than to Danny. He was also thinking that the surest way to excite pursuit was to run away—

They rode on through the early afternoon, the sun's rays blinding as it reflected from the dust-dry mesa. As they rode they kept watch for the party ahead, hoping to see it in time to avoid it.

At last they came out on a brief hill overlooking

the town. Careless reined in and the others halted beside him. He shoved back his stained hat and peered through the heat haze that made the squat little town on the edge of the river shimmer in a fantasy of distortion.

He turned to Danny Pugh. His big face registered puzzlement. 'That's queer,' he growled. 'There's no fightin' in the town, jes' people walkin' about. What's happened to the Big Mouth and his gang?'

A man answered that question for them. He had been in hiding behind an outcrop of basalt, but now, recognising them, he came walking slowly forward, leading his horse.

Danny called 'Dad!' delightedly, and jumped down to meet the old man.

Careless watched that old, worn face and noted the drooping, almost lifeless gait and his heart sank. So he got down, too, and walked over after the boy.

Over the kid's shoulder he asked, softly, 'Trouble Joe?'

Bleak grey eyes lifted to his. That old head nodded. 'Yeah, trouble. Plenty trouble, Careless.'

So Careless led him away so as to listen to him while the boys prepared coffee. The story came out. There had been treachery after the coach had left to make the run to Neuces Bend.

'Some o' the fellars thought ter save their own hides,' Joe told him. 'They went an' got Fergie and the others out the barn where they'd bin put – gave 'em guns an' backed 'em in takin' charge of the town again!'

140

ELEVEN

THE CHARGING ARMY!

Careless breathed, 'Wal, ef that don't beat the band!'

Joe said tiredly, 'First thing we knew of it, there they were, right behind us. We put up a bit of a fight, but we didn't know who'd gone over to the enemy an' who was still on our side, and so we started to run for it.

'A few of us got hurt, a lot got captured, but a dozen or so of us got away. The last I saw of Carlos an' some of the men was them swimmin' the river. I lit out across the mesa, hid when I saw the Big Mouth ride right up to the town, then came on towards Neuces Bend.'

'Then you saw us an' holed up agen?'

The old man nodded. Then, despairingly, he asked, 'What're we gonna do, big fellar?'

Careless just shrugged and said, helplessly, 'Old-timer, I jes' don't have an idea. Let's see if some coffee'll help?'

They squatted around the tiny fire, drinking the hot, black, sugarless liquid. While they drank they talked, and in time Careless began to work himself out of that feeling of helplessness.

The boys were all for rounding up as many friends as possible and making a night attack on the town.

'You think you c'n drive the Big Mouth an' his friends outa Broken Knee – you an' a coupla dozen other rannies?' Old Joseph Pugh's lip curled with contempt. He was feeling a lot better now, after that coffee, but he still couldn't feel optimistic.

Careless was moving across to his patient horse, which was standing close to the shade of the basalt outcrop, its tail swishing against the assaults of a host of vicious flies.

Pugh called softly, 'You're up ter something, Careless. Won't you tell a fellar?'

Careless' face was impassive. He didn't want to arouse vain hope. 'I'm jes' goin' scoutin' up that butte,' he told him. 'Mebbe I'll think o' somethin' in that time. Meanwhile, you fellars keep off the skyline an' stay here till I come back.'

With that he rode away.

The hours passed slowly for the men within that

screen of rock on the little hill just off the trail. The horses appreciated the rest, recovering from their night's fatigue, and nibbling at the sparse grass that somehow managed to survive even in that rainless near-desert.

But the boys, and old Joseph Pugh, were restless and uneasy with the long wait. They lay around and lounged about and looked hopefully westward where the giant buttes reared, and the time dragged until it seemed to be standing still.

Still Careless O'Connor didn't come. They became anxious and after a couple of hours some of the boys were for tracking after the big fellar to see if he had run into trouble. Old Joseph counselled against this, however.

'Careless said for us to dig in an' wait, an' Careless knows what he's talkin' about,' he argued. 'We'll hole up until nightfall, anyway. He'll be back soon, you bet.'

But it was another rider who eventually rode up to them. They saw him far out on the mesa, riding like fury, his horse's mane and tail streaming in the wind, a cloud of dust kicking up behind.

At first they thought it might be the saddle tramp, but after a while they were able to see that this rider wore a grey shirt, not the flamboyant coloured one of O'Connor's.

Old Joe, watching through narrowed eyes, opined, 'The way that fellar rides, there's trouble comin' fer someone – fast. No man rides a hoss like that unless it's matter o' life an' death.'

'Mebbe,' his son opined in return, 'someone's goin' ter mean us.'

It was. When he had climbed the short hill, the rider unhesitatingly plunged off among the rocky piles towards their hiding place.

Joe stepped out, guns up and covering him. The rider flung up one hand to show his peaceable mission, and dragged his horse to a sudden stop. They recognised him. It was one of the young men from Neuces Bend – young Yippee Clay, who had lately taken to stagecoach riding.

Joe shoved his guns away at once. 'What's wrong?' he demanded. 'Trouble?'

Burt shouted, 'Don't talk! Git your hosses and beat it away from this trail right now!' The boys started to jump for their horses, recognising the urgency in the lean young Texan's voice. As they leapt into their saddles they heard him cry a further instruction, 'Swim the Neuces an' rendezvous among the pines right opposite Broken Knee. Now – git goin'. It's every man for himself!'

They went away like the wind, racing frantically for the distant river bank, three miles away. They didn't know what they were running from, but they didn't stop to ask questions.

For they knew that though Burt gave the orders, the man behind them was big Careless O'Connor – and Careless didn't give orders for nothing.

Burt and old Joseph brought up the rear. The old-timer noticed that Burt kept glancing back towards the trail they had just left, as if anxious about something. He seemed relieved when they gained the brown, sullen waters of the broad Neuces before seeing anyone back along that distant trail. A few men appeared on the trail sending bullets after them, too late to have any effect.

In silence they swam their panting horses to the far bank, and then they rested before riding on to the pines. The force of the current had separated them as they swam, so that the boys were strung out over half a mile, and it made Burt uneasy, for they had been brought within sight of the enemy-occupied Broken Knee.

As they jogged inland towards the distant black patch of tall pines, Joe asked dryly, 'Mebbe now you'll tell us why you set us ter runnin' like skeered gophers?'

Burt shrugged. 'I don't know myself. All I know is that Careless came ridin' into Neuces Bend so fast he came nigh near ter flyin' fer the first time in his life!' He fumbled for the makings and started to roll a curly. 'He jes' hollered fer me ter git you all off that trail faster'n fast – told me where you were an' what ter tell you. An' that's all I know,' he ended.

The boys gradually drew together and then disappeared one by one into the coolness of the pine knoll. In a glade they dismounted and unsaddled, pretty sure they were safe on this side of the river. Old Joseph said he'd ride on later and try to track Carlos and the others who had crossed the river when the Big Mouth returned.

They saw a great cloud of dust billowing on the trail about a mile beyond the dozing cattle town. Almost at once, faintly over the water they heard the cries of the men inside Broken Knee, and they saw them rushing about in what seemed like great confusion.

That billowing cloud drew nearer, a great rolling mass of grey-white dust from the alkali desert. It came to within a few hundred yards of the town before the boys across the river saw the cause of it.

Then they gasped with astonishment.

For there was an army charging savagely on into Broken Knee, hundreds of wild horsemen, nearly naked – and wearing the sombrero of Mexico.

'Mexicans!' they shouted. 'What on earth—'

They couldn't believe their eyes. Here were three or four hundred raiders, miles north of the Border, attacking a Texas town in broad daylight. It didn't seem possible!

It probably seemed just as incredible to the Crooked S rannies who occupied the town, too, but the raw voice of the Big Mouth, exulting in spite of the danger, drove them out of their stunned astonishment.

Right across the river that big, bellowing thunder of a voice carried, so that without any trouble they could hear the orders he gave.

His rannies leapt into action. They ran to the buildings that rimmed the tiny town and opened vicious rifle fire on the charging Mexicans – others

broke out cases of ammunition and went stagger-
ing up with great loads to distribute to the defenders.

The Mexicans were driven back by that first blast
of fire. The Texans' rifles were too deadly for them.
But they were determined, and now they came
back to the attack on their stomachs, abandoning
their ponies and crawling from cover to cover and
all the while closing in on the hated gringos.

Old Joseph, watching across the river, said,
'They'll take the town, after dark, them Mexes.'
His face was gloomy. 'That means there won't be
any town fer us to go back to,' he ended.

'Nope.' It was his son, Danny, a wiser man now
than he'd been before going off with the filibusters. 'They'll fire the place, them Mexes, just as
the Big Mouth would have done to that village with
the Spanish mission, after it had been looted.'

Old Joseph spat tobacco juice. 'It's as Careless
says,' he told them. 'We settlers have ter foot the
bill fer the murderin' misdeeds o' people like the
Big Mouth.' Then he sighed, because Broken
Knee was his home and the home of his people,
and if it went up in flames he'd have to start all
over again. 'An' I'm gettin' too old ter start from
scratch, like I've done times before,' he thought.

Despair gripped the old man, watching the
savage battle across the Neuces River. It made him
feel bad, to have to lie up in hiding and not take
any part in the defence of his own property. But
what was there he could do, with only a handful of

young men to help him?

A few minutes later one of the boys called out, 'Look, there's someone swimmin' the river towards us!'

Joseph lifted his head and saw the bobbing black dot. Then he saw another behind it, and another. Within minutes there were thirty or forty men swimming the river, and they were being swept right across towards where they lay in the pine grove.

Joseph could think of only one thing. 'Looks like some o' the rats are pullin' out. Mebbe they c'n see, too, that sooner or later them Mexes is gonna bust that town wide open, an' mebbe roast 'em in the ruins when they've done it.'

The boys got out their guns and waited, crouching, ready to jump forward and cover the swimmers as they staggered ashore. The first man was coming in – so near they could hear his gasping breath. Joseph was about to give the order to reveal themselves when suddenly they found themselves surrounded by close on fifty mounted men, who had stolen into the copse while their attention was occupied across the river.

TWELVE

NICE LITTLE DOVE!

Joseph let out a startled yell, and all the boys came jumping to their feet. Then one of the men came spurring forward, shouting, 'Put up your guns! It's me, 'Connor!'

Old Joe let out a sigh of relief. Then he pointed to the men coming out of the water. 'Watch out,' he shouted, 'them varmints is escapin' from the town.'

But Careless just dismounted, shaking his head and grinning. He called back, 'They're your friends, Joe. I sent young Jim Whitfield into the town down the edge of the river. He was to pass the word around ter let the Crooked S bunch fight this out among themselves. Here they come now – an' Jim's among them,' he exclaimed gladly. He liked Grace's headstrong but courageous brother.

Joe looked curiously at the men who were dismounting behind their leader. He saw Carlos and about a dozen others of the townspeople, and he ran forward to shake their hands. He was overjoyed to find them alive.

'We went the long way round into Neuces Bend,' they told Joseph. 'Gee, it was a long walk. An' when we got there, Careless found hosses for us an' rode us straightway back with some of the Neuces Bend men who offered ter give a hand in the fightin' tonight.'

'Fightin' tonight? echoed the old-timer. 'I didn't know there was goin' ter be any, 'cept between the Mexes an' the Big Mouth's doggone gunnies!'

'Yeah,' said Careless, pushing up to them. 'There's gonna be fightin' tonight, Joe, old-timer. You don't think we're gonna lose the town to Simms or to the Mexican fire-raisers, do you?'

The news electrified the men. They were instantly jubilant to think that their homes were going to be saved, and it was pathetic the way they showed their trust in the big, flat-faced *hombre* who stood grinning at them.

The men came walking across from out of the river, now – about forty of them, all told. Jim Whitfield came up dripping, to report that all who could swim had obeyed Careless' order to come across.

'There's plenty left who couldn't swim,' he added, 'but I passed the word around to watch out for our arrival after dark.'

That was all the news the men there needed. They were to cross the river after dark and enter the town. 'What we're goin' ter do,' Careless told them, 'is shove the Big Mouth an' his men right out of the town on to the mesa.' He shrugged. 'They c'n fight it out there with the Mexes; they brought it on themselves, anyway.'

They had two hours to wait for dusk, so they settled down to watch the fighting in the town opposite. The sound of firing was heavy and continuous, and the white gunpowder smoke drifted in heavy banks over the river towards them. In time they even got to smelling the biting odor of the smoke.

It was difficult now to see the Mexicans, who were advancing with painful slowness through the scrub and rock-strewn prairie towards the heavily defended buildings on the outskirts of the town. That was obvious, though – that the Mexicans were advancing.

'They're out fer blood,' someone said.

'Yeah,' growled one of the kids who had been across the Border with the filibusters. 'I reckon this mob's the one we saw formin' up outside the Mex village with that Spanish mission in the centre of it. I don't blame 'em fer wantin' ter put finish ter the Big Mouth. He's done so much damage with his filibusterin' expeditions, I reckon they figger they've got ter stop him right here an' now.'

Old Joseph growled, 'I ain't agen 'em fer that, but – wal, it's gonna cost us a packet, especially if them Mexes manage ter get into the town, as they will after dark.'

'We'll get there before 'em,' Careless smiled confidently.

Then Danny Pugh got to asking questions.

'Hey, there, you big fellar, there's a lot you c'n tell us before we swim that river agen.'

'Such as?'

'How come them Mexes knew ter come ter Broken Knee? We left a blind trail pointin' towards Neuces Bend. Why didn't they head that way, as the Big Mouth nacherly expected 'em to do?'

So big Careless O'Connor sat down and did a bit of talking. 'I figgered the Mexes might come trackin' after the filibusters,' he drawled. 'What I didn't expect was that they'd come so quickly.

'When I got up on top o' that bluff I could see as far as the Rio Grande, and the Mexes were already on the north bank. I hadn't time ter get back an' warn you fellars, so I jes' hightailed it into Neuces Bend to give warnin'. I sent Yippee along ter get you off the trail, outa the Mexican's way, then went back with a few men to wipe out the false trail that led straight on to Broken Knee.'

It sounded so easy; it certainly explained everything. And Careless' quick-wittedness tickled the humour of those crude Westerners and they sat back and guffawed with delight. The Big Mouth had been neatly outwitted, and was now having to suffer the consequences of his evil acts.

Then Careless told the little group something else, and now he wasn't grinning.

'There's bin a lot of hard things said about me,' he told them. 'Words like renegade and traitor have bin thrown at me. Wal, I reckon no man likes to hear sich things said agen his character, an' I wanted ter prove to you how wrong it all was. Only I couldn't.'

'Why not, Careless?' someone asked when he paused.

Careless played with the dry sand between his feet, sifting it through his strong brown fingers. 'Because I'd have been useless in my job ef you'd known who I was – am,' he corrected. He stood up. Now they could see how much he had suffered in having to remain silent while those charges were hurled at him.

'I did a lot of good work around Oaxaco in gettin' the Mexicans to lay down their arms to the Rangers,' he went on. 'I got a lot of credit fer that. So, when the Rangers were asked for a man with Border knowledge for a special job, they picked on me.

'Nobody knew what the job was – neither did I, until I reached Galveston by ship. Then they told me I had to find the ringleader of a band of filibusters who were threatening the peace along the Border. They had no Rangers to post along the Border to stop the trouble, so they deputed me ter find out who was behind it all – an' settle it my own way.'

He looked grimly across the brown, sullen Neuces River.

'Wal, there's the Big Mouth – a fellar I opine ter meet fer the first time soon – the filibuster chief himself, trapped in Broken Knee. I sure am settlin' it my own way,' he ended tersely.

Old Joseph sighed. 'You sure are, Careless. The Big Mouth's trapped like a nut in a crackerjack – ef the Mexes don't get their revenge on him, we'll fix his hide fer him!'

Two hours later they slipped into the water, guns and cartridge belts tied on to their heads to keep them dry. It was nearly night, but there was a big moon rising, promising to give a light as bright, almost, as day.

The battle sounded to have worked up to a fury of activity in the last quarter of an hour, as if the Mexicans were closing in and attacking the defenders with greater vigour. Everywhere they saw the red flashes of the Mexicans' rifles as they came crawling in over the mesa – heard the crackle of rifles and the shorter, duller boom as Colts came into play. That alone told how close the Mexicans were to the town now

Swimming strongly, big Careless urged them into faster speed. 'We've got to take hold of the town afore them Mexes get a foothold,' he told them, and at that everyone swam with renewed vigour.

They came out where an old wharf lay. It was used when a shallow draft boat came up from Corpus Christi, after the spring floods had given depth to the shallows twenty or thirty miles east of the town. Careless pulled himself up cautiously and then flitted over the moonlit open space into the shadows. Here he buckled on his guns and waited for his followers to straggle out after him.

While he waited he heard shouting from inside a big warehouse. He sent some of the first arrivals across to find out what it signified. One of the men came quickly back to say it was the rest of the citizens, the men who couldn't swim; the Big Mouth had locked them away in order to prevent them from deserting and crossing to the west bank of the Neuces River after their comrades.

'Tell 'em to pick up what weapons they can an' jine us,' Careless ordered, and then he began to creep across to where an alley emptied off the plaza, just by the gambling saloon that Fergie Allbright owned.

There were men in the buildings, firing out at the red flashes on the mesa. They'd be the Crooked S rannies, Careless thought, and then he went jumping forward, guns blazing.

It demoralised the Broken Knee defenders, that vicious rush from the rear, and it had a curious effect upon the Mexicans. Their firing slackened, as if they were uncertain of the identity of the attackers.

Before the Crooked S men knew what was happening, they had been driven from the buildings and were being herded down the moonlit alley towards the watching Mexicans on the mesa.

They didn't go easily. They fought back ferociously, knowing their fate if they got pushed out beyond the buildings and into the arms of the Mexicans. It was a ding-dong battle, but now the returned settlers were in greater force, and they were fighting for their existence. They marched forward relentlessly, and inexorably the filibusters were driven down the alley.

The fight seemed to take hours, but probably only lasted a minute or two, so fierce was the barrage of fire put up by Careless' men. And much the same was happening along the other alleys that led out of the plaza, Careless knew.

Careless heard someone call out that Fergie Allbright had given himself up. 'He's yaller,' a contemptuous voice shouted. 'He didn't try to fight with the others!'

For a time, too, Careless heard the savage, bull-like bellow of the Big Mouth in a distant alley, as he rallied his men and at the same time hurled abuse at the new enemy. Hearing that raving voice, Careless thought the fellow couldn't be right in his head.

Then the voice was silent. Everyone wondered if a bullet had silenced the filibuster leader, but there was no time for speculation, for the filibusters were falling away in disorder suddenly, as if the absence of their leader's presence left them in a panic.

There was a lull in the fighting after that, and then the Mexicans came storming towards the town. They were repulsed by the settlers in a way that must have shaken the attackers, for after milling around for some time across the plain, they began slowly to withdraw along the Border trail. To find a new, strongly ensconced enemy, just in the moment of victory, probably knocked all the heart out of them.

Careless posted a patrol out on the mesa, to give warning in case the Mexicans returned, then everyone began to attend to the wounded and bring them in to the comforts of their beds. The settlers had got off lightly, but the gunmen had suffered a terrible defeat, and there was scarcely a one who wasn't wounded.

But the Big Mouth, the dreaded enemy, the filibuster chief himself, wasn't to be found either among the dead or the wounded, and Careless gave orders for a search to be made for him.

He walked his horse down towards the wharf, leading it by the reins. He had a feeling that a man wanting to escape would probably choose the river way out and swim for the far bank. 'Mebbe he's a mile away by now,' Careless was thinking, when a stir in the darkness sent his hand rocketing toward his Colt.

A little old man with a high bald head came blinking out into the moonlight.

Careless called, 'Better watch out, fellar. The Big Mouth's supposed ter be still in town.'

The nearest searchers were fifty yards away. He turned to look back at them. The little, craggy-beaked old man hit him from behind and stretched him stunned on the ground. Then he jumped on to the horse and sent it bolting up the moonlit alley.

Dazed, but recovering rapidly, Careless staggered to his feet and looked after that horse with its tiny rider. He didn't understand – yet.

Then that little rider let out a shout of triumph at his cleverness, and the voice that floated back to Careless was like a tidal wave of brutal, offensive sound. Then he understood.

For once, Careless had been outwitted. For once he had erred.

That little rider was the Big Mouth himself!

'The tarnation!' Careless exclaimed in wrath, running after the fleeing horse and rider. 'He's gonna get away!'

And he blamed himself for it. Then his humour returned, at the thought of how the tables had been turned on him. He'd never seen the Big Mouth and so didn't recognise him when he stepped from the shadows. And somehow, because of the name and swashbuckling reputation, he'd always expected David Simms to be a big, gross creature.

Instead of which he was spare, short, old and bald-headed.

'How was I to know?' he consoled himself, and then he paused, listening. There was a sudden crackle of rifle fire, far out on the mesa, in the direction the Big Mouth had just taken.

Some men came running up to Careless' side. They all listened, but there was silence now on the mesa. Then Careless said, slowly, 'I reckon that was the Big Mouth. I reckon he escaped us only ter run slap bang into a bunch o' Mexes.' He sighed. 'If there's any consolation,' he said, 'it is ter think that a Mexican settled a lot of scores with his gun, just then.'

They didn't see Careless after first light next morning. And only one man saw him ride away westwards, towards the Border hills. He was Burt Clay, a fine young Texan who was like a child in his sorrow when Ben and Jim Whitfield found him later.

'He's gone,' the lean young puncher told them. 'Careless. He's hit the trail, 'cause he said his work's finished here an' there's another job for him ter do near Del Rio. He gave me his share in the stage-line partnership. I'm kinda fifty-fifty with Grace now.'

His foot scuffed awkwardly in the dirt.

'You know what he said?' His eyes came up hopefully to the two other men. 'He said, "You're the fellar fer Gracie, Burt. You jes' ask her when you ride in an' see".' He paused again, and now he was uncertain. Wistfully his voice asked, 'What d'you think, fellars? Think the old tramp's right?'

Ben looked at Jim, scratched his head and thought for a while. And then he said, 'You know, Burt, mebbe he is at that. You know somep'n – I ain't never known the old rogue wrong yet!'

And the old rogue was right, when Burt came to asking his question of Grace.